Folklore From the Herts

THE HERTFORDSHIRE WRITING GROUP   MIMI BROWN

TAYLOR MCLEOD   S. VALENTINE ASTORIA

CALUM DICKINSON   EMILY SIGGERS

STUART WAKEFIELD   EMMA TURNER

write-hearted books

Introduction

The Hertfordshire Writing Group is an open and supportive community united in their journey to hone their writing skills and keep the creative flames burning all year round. Our meetings buzz with energy, brimming with fresh ideas and insights, making it the perfect incubator for creative projects.

In the spirit of this continued collaboration and diversity, we embraced the challenge of curating our *second* anthology. As before, we sought a unifying theme that resonates with all. This led us to the enchanting realm of folklore—a timeless tapestry woven from the threads of myths, legends, and cultural tales that have shaped human experience for generations. Like folklore, each writer's voice is unique, yet together, they create a harmonious blend of narrative magic.

It is with immense pleasure that I introduce *Folklore From the Herts*. This collection is a celebration of our county's storytelling talent, each writer bringing their distinct flair while remaining committed to their personal best.

Enjoy the journey into the mythical and the magical.

Stuart Wakefield

For more about The Hertfordshire Writing Group and our projects, please visit www.facebook.com/groups/hertswritinggroup

Contents

The Future of the (Once) King

L egends often tell of heroes, their rise and fall, their victory, and their loss. This one speaks of the aftermath of greatness. A land of apples and a once broken blade, reforged but blunted, kept from its wielders. The new chapter of a book once closed. A melody sung by an unpractised yet eager young man, who even now feels drawn to something brilliant, something beyond all he knows. Drawn to the epilogue of a legend, and to a voice which speaks only to him.

~

BENEATH THE WHITE BLOSSOMS OF A hawthorn, Arthur watched the fishermen set sail with an undisguised envy. Not that he fancied himself a seafarer. He had once, as a boy. But growing up on the island had allowed him to bear witness to the harsh realities of the ocean: he had seen enough to wish his own encounters with its treacherous depths to be brief. All the same, he envied those fishermen - for their freedom.

His island was a small one, a few hundred inhabitants, few enough that you could be known at a glance, or at least recognised for the bloodline you heralded from. Arthur himself bore little resemblance to most of his family, but many claimed they saw his aunt in him, or at least her mischief.

Apparently, she had once snuck aboard a fishing vessel as a child, just to get a closer look at the isles beyond their own. He had tried to speak with her about it, once, but his parents had quickly put an end to that line of questioning. After all, the people of this isle didn't speak of the beyond.

Arthur couldn't understand it. How could his people be so content to exist in a place whose greatest boast was some apples and a fancy sword? A sword that may not even have existed, since no one Arthur had met had ever seen it first-hand. In fact, most of the tales about it ended with some idiot throwing it into a lake. Didn't sound like a particularly fancy sword to him if it could be discarded so easily.

Turning from the bay as the tiny fishing boats disappeared from sight, Arthur settled down beneath the burgeoning awning, grimacing a little as the movement urged the pungent smell of white and purple buds to hover in the air around him. Garlic. Arthur would *never* understand the island's fascination with it.

Closing his eyes, he attempted to tune out the odour, musing instead, as he often did, about the sights those fishermen might see beyond the bounds of this land. Were there trees in the beyond too? Towering great monuments that stretched high enough to block out the stars. Or tiny little stumps, barely peering from the earth. He hoped there was less garlic. Maybe a few apples. And swords. Fancier swords than this place could ever *dream* of.

Sometimes he fancied he could hear whispers when he lay beneath these branches. Whispers that were familiar, but not, coaxing him beyond his cradle of allium and thorn to the world beyond these waters...

He wondered if those whispers came from someone. If there were more people beyond this isle. He believed there were. Hundreds more. Thousands even. Enough that he could be utterly unknown. That he could disappear amidst a crowd. That someone could see him without seeing a relative or an echo of someone else in his place. Just see him. Just Arthur.

He was drawn from his thoughts by the sensation of being watched.

At the base of the tree stood a pale woman. Quiet. Almost unnaturally so. After all, he had not heard her approach, with only the breeze and a few crickets to muffle her steps. How long had she been standing there? He realised he might be staring a little *too* intently, but it was difficult to look away. She was... unlike anyone he'd ever seen.

Her pallor was comparable to that of the blossoms which surrounded her feet. Yet, before his eyes, those blossoms seemed to fade, curling in upon themselves until only a husk remained. This woman seemed to carry autumn's gifts in her wake. Her hand brushed the bark of the tree and haws sprouted amidst the blossoms, tainting their purity. She sighed and across the breeze came the scent of spice... and rot. Even the hawthorns seemed to quake in her presence. Yet all of this was quickly forgotten once he met her gaze.

Her eyes... darker than the blackest night, deeper than the most treacherous ocean. There were terrible truths hidden in those eyes, ones his mind simultaneously struggled to grasp and recoiled from. The knowledge in those chasms was not the kind to be unlearnt.

"Arthur." His eyes widened. She *knew* him. A stranger. From the beyond? She'd have to be. Her garments, haggard as they were, clearly were not of the island. *She* was not of this island. His curiosity suddenly overrode his fear. Could it be her whose whispers he had heard?

"Yes, I am Arthur... who are you?" The woman's eyes, previously expressionless, turned sad at his words. An ashen hand reached out to brush his cheek. It was all Arthur could do to resist the urge to recoil from it.

"Who I am matters not."

"It matters to me." Even the wind seemed silent as it awaited her response.

"I have been known by many names, but Igraine is the one which best suits me now, since I cannot be what I once was." She brushed her hand through Arthur's hair, softer than the blossoms beneath her feet.

"And what was that?"

The woman's gaze briefly turned from him, towards a single lone hut atop the sands. His aunt's home.

"A mother."

For a moment Arthur wondered if the woman before him was his grandmother, before reminding himself that said woman was considerably shorter and less... well, *affectionate* than this woman appeared to be. She'd always been especially cold towards the two of them, given their inclination towards the beyond. But this woman? Now when she turned her gaze back towards Arthur, it was as if he held all the answers to the universe. It was... overwhelming, especially from a woman he'd just met.

Perhaps she saw this in his gaze because moments later she removed her hand from his hair, stepping away to observe the horizon the fishermen had disappeared beyond.

"As I spoke before, who I am matters not. I am simply here as a messenger."

"A messenger? For who?" Anyone on the isle could deliver their own messages easily enough so... someone from the beyond? The voice? Something in her stance told him this was one answer he wouldn't be receiving. "What's the message?"

"My message is this. The voice which calls you does so for a reason..." She paused, turning back to face Arthur. "Do *not* answer it." A sudden chill settled in the air and Arthur got the distinct impression that the horrible knowledge in this woman's eyes was linked intrinsically to that voice... He wished he could say it dimmed his curiosity about the speaker.

"Who is it? Why can't I answer?" But Igraine was

silent. And before Arthur could scramble to his feet, she dissipated before him like a fine woman-shaped, mist. "Igraine!" There was no response, save the soft caress of an invisible hand, ruffling his hair.

ARTHUR SPENT THE BETTER PART OF THE following two weeks seeking out the woman he'd met, despite his suspicions that the search would fail to yield any results. After all, a woman like her, one who looked beyond the horizon and spoke of it, could not belong to this isle... and he knew of no other women who could turn to mist.

All the same, he searched through journals and logs, scoured the streets, and even spoke to the elders of his encounter... Most dismissed his ramblings as the dreams of a youthful and idle mind, though one of the eldest, a grave man known as Harker, had pulled Arthur aside and handed him a small vial of something to use 'in case her, or other such apparitions return'. Then again, Harker was known as the isle's eccentric so perhaps being believed by him had been the reason the rest had dismissed him so easily.

He'd tried to peer inside the vial once, only to find a clear odourless substance, not all that dissimilar to water. In fact, it might have *been* water, knowing Harker. All the same, he couldn't be sure. He kept the vial but resolved not to use it for now. After all, whatever Igraine might be, she hadn't appeared to be a threat.

And yet something told him the voice she'd warned him against wasn't either. At least, not to him.

With all other avenues he tried failing to yield results, Arthur had reluctantly resigned himself to the idea that Igraine would become yet another intangible mystery from the beyond when suddenly he recalled her odd fixation on a lone hut while they'd spoken. A hut belonging to a certain aunt of his...

With little further thought, Arthur headed to the shores. The fishermen weren't due back for days so no one would be there to witness if he strayed beyond the socially acceptable borders of their society, where the seemingly endless fields of pungent white and purple ended, and the sands began. Where *she* lived.

Arthur waded through the coarse sands, scooping up a shell or two as an offering he knew his aunt would appreciate, before tentatively knocking on the door.

Moments later, he was forced to launch himself into the sands to avoid the swift swing of wooden panels. Behind them stood a woman whose eyes held a little of the beyond and a lot of the mischief she was known for. A bright-eyed woman with hair that flowed like the waves she was so fond of. And with features and a smile so strikingly like Arthur's, he knew his own existence had been the subject of more than one scandal for his grandmother, since many had believed them to be siblings... Come to think of it, perhaps *that* was why she wasn't that affectionate.

Of course, none of this had been helped by his aunt's own amusement regarding the scandals. Which was why she called him, "Little brother! I see you snuck away from the village again to see your favourite big sis."

"You're my only big sis." So maybe *he* found the scandals funny too... Besides, he'd never particularly enjoyed being an only child. He couldn't help but feel that was *incorrect* somehow. All he knew was that calling his aunt his sibling felt *right*.

"Which makes me your favourite." She teased as she helped Arthur up from the beach.

"For lack of any better options, congratulations on your uncontested victory."

"A victory is a victory kid; you'll learn not to take those for granted soon enough." She ruffled his hair, laughing at the grimace it produced on Arthur's face.

"I think I liked it better when you called me little

brother." He mumbled as he followed her inside the hut.

"You *are* a kid Arthur. Especially with the way my sister coddles you."

Arthur made a face. "And she's not wrong either, knowing what you're like."

"And what am I like?" His aunt's smile slipped slightly.

"Like me." Arthur wasn't quite sure what to make of that, so he offered up the shells he'd gathered instead. She accepted them with a fond smile, ruffling his hair before she accepted them in a way that was remarkably similar to Igraine... The odd wistful feeling in the air receded as his curiosity returned.

"Hey Mor, do you know someone called Igraine?" His aunt froze. "You do, don't you?"

"I wouldn't exactly call it *knowing*..."

"But you've seen her?"

"Once. Many years ago... I would've been no more than ten. A child... She must be older than Harker now."

"She wasn't."

"Maybe a daughter of hers then... Was she about your age?"

"Older." His aunt seemed unsettled by this.

"It's probably just a common name..."

"But it isn't. I've never met anyone else with that name before. Not here... I don't think she was from here Mor." His aunt's gaze grew distant, as if seeing something he couldn't.

"Yes, I don't suppose she was..." Her eyes suddenly snapped to his, "What did she say?"

"She said her name was Igraine. That she used to be a mother? And-" He hesitated. The voice was personal, was his. Might not even be *real*, despite what the woman had said. He wasn't sure he wanted to share it, even with his aunt.

"And?"

"She knew my name."

"She knew mine too." He stared at his aunt, surprised. "She found me one day, playing by the shoreline. I'd snuck out while your grandparents weren't looking. And she found me. She said 'Morgana, I know the mysteries whose answers you seek. But in seeking those answers, all you will unearth is pain.'" Arthur couldn't help but notice the similarities between Igraine's words to Morgana and to him. Both messages were warnings.

"Did you listen to her?" Morgana laughed.

"When have I ever listened to anyone? Four years later I snuck away on a boat to find the very answers she warned me against."

"And? Did you find them?" Her mirth seemed to flicker out and fade.

"In many ways, I did… Did she say anything else?" Arthur considered this for a moment before shaking his head. "Well, she hardly seems the type to follow one set of rules. Perhaps she'll return and tell you the reason for your meeting then." She offered Arthur a fond smile, "She seemed lonely when I met her, and I know first-hand that you happen to make excellent company."

Arthur offered a smile back, watching as Morgana returned to the task of organising the new shells he'd gathered. Which was why her next words caught him so off guard. "You're not going to listen to her either, are you?"

"…Probably not."

"Well, I can hardly begrudge you for making my own mistakes." She set the final shell in place before turning back to face Arthur. "Promise you'll at least come to say goodbye before leaving?"

"I promise."

THAT NIGHT SLEEP FELL UPON ARTHUR AS snow falls upon hawthorn, heavy but inclined to collapse at any given moment. His dreams were fragmented. Little girls with boats, women with haunted eyes and soft hands, the overwhelming scent of garlic, swords in lakes, horses, ornate buildings with high walls and turrets, a woman wearing a circlet of gold, a crowd bowing, swords, fighting, someone screaming and beneath it all, a whisper. Soft but certain.

Arthur. Come to us Arthur. We all wait for you.

Eyes. Old, wise, dark. A smile. Familiar and not.

Arthur.

He awoke in a frenzy of tangled sheets, slipping to the floor with a lack of dignity he could only be grateful no one was there to witness. The series of images, already intangible to him in the way all dreams are, faded. As usual, the whisper lingered. It was fainter now. But if he *really* focused, he could still hear it.

Arthur. I wait for you.

Oddly enough, even in a whisper he could hear the yearning behind those words. It made him want to whisper back. Perhaps he would've if he believed the voice would actually hear... Well, that and Igraine's warning still rang clear in his mind. *Do not answer back.*

He decided to distract himself, musing instead on what it was Morgana had seen. Which answers she could've found all those years ago that would still cause her to look so haunted all these years later. Something from the beyond, he supposed. Something terrible.

But not his voice. He knew with certainty that it couldn't be. That this voice would protect him. He'd always known that, somehow. From the second he first heard it speak.

Arthur.

They were waiting. The voice and whoever else was with them. He couldn't keep them waiting much longer. He'd been patient enough, he thought. Waited a lot longer than his aunt did to seek answers, despite her insistence that he was still a kid. Eighteen was *not* the age of a kid. He was ready, or at least as ready as he could be growing up on an island that refused to speak of the world beyond.

Arthur.

He was ready. He *had* to be.

IT TURNED OUT SNEAKING FROM HIS HOME, a bag of essentials and a few other provisions in tow, was a *lot* easier than he'd expected. Perhaps it could be attributed to the odd sense of distance he'd always felt between him and his parents. They hadn't been *bad* as such. Had raised him well, cared for him. He hadn't been neglected or lonely but... all the same, he'd never quite felt that connection, the same way he did with Morgana or the voice. Much like his absence of a sibling, something about his parents had always felt... *off* somehow.

Perhaps they'd felt that same unnaturalness.

Rather than ponder his good fortune, Arthur chose to seize the opportunity, hurrying back to the shores where Morgana's hut awaited.

Oddly enough, she seemed to anticipate his arrival. She stood, eyes to the horizon, the ocean lapping at her feet. In her hands she clutched something, Arthur wasn't quite sure what, though his attention quickly turned from both his aunt and the object when he noticed something infinitely more valuable.

"You brought me a boat?"

"You take after me in many ways, little bro, but you never quite inherited my capacity for stealth... Figured you'd get a lot further if you didn't have to swim to the mainland." Arthur grinned at her, moving to settle his belongings in the boat. "Sail east, that way the wind will guide your journey... though something tells me you could sail directly into the storm and still find your way."

"Because I'm like you?"

Morgana laughed, the sound a muted version of

her usual mirth. "No. Because *he* wouldn't allow it to be any other way."

The voice. Something inside Arthur knew it *had* to be the voice she referred to. He really would keep Arthur safe then. If Morgana believed it too, then there was no reason to doubt it.

So why did the thought of actually boarding this boat and sailing away still fill him with dread?

"You'll be okay Arthur."

"Come with me?" The words surprised him, and her too if her reaction was anything to go by. Still, he persisted. "You said it yourself, I'm great company. You'll miss me."

"That was never in doubt." She pulled him into a tight hug. A little *too* tight. "Arthur... Did I ever tell you the story of the woman and the water?" Arthur was caught off guard by the abrupt change of subject.

"I... don't think so?" She pulled back, her eyes wistful as she guided him to sit.

"Once upon a time there was a woman. Or at least she considered herself as such. After all, she could hardly still be considered a girl at her age. She had lived ten summers in this world, far more than her sister could boast at her measly five. She knew she was ready for great adventures and that such adventures awaited her, if only she took to the water. You see, she had always felt a calling to the waves. Like the ocean itself lived within her heart, urging her forward so the two could become whole... sometimes it even seemed to *speak*."

Arthur did his best not to show his discomfort at her words. But how could he not feel unsettled? The ocean *speaking*? Specifically to *her*? Almost like... No. It couldn't be the same voice. That voice was *his*. He *knew* that. And the woman sounded so distinctly like his aunt. Was *this* how she was choosing to tell him what she'd seen in the beyond?

"So, one day she followed the voice, letting it carry her to the waves. She stepped aboard a vessel belonging to a grumpy old man who bore little notice to a stow-away. Below the deck she clambered, watching the world eagerly as it approached through bars of mahogany. The world which had called to her so desperately. The *beyond*.

"But then came what the woman could not predict. Then came the roaring from beneath. Then came the waves and the battle the valiant steed she had boarded could not outrun. Then came the sound of a not quite scream, swallowed by the winds... And then came the world. The world she should have forgotten. The world that had not forgotten her. The world that made sure she would never forget again."

Her hand idly brushed an old scar. One Arthur had noticed once or twice in his youth but had never thought much of. Two thin marks. Like pricks from an oversized needle. Perfectly parallel and precise... oddly so. He had asked her once, what these marks were from. She laughed, as she so often did, and replied 'from my greatest adventure'. Now that he thought about it, he was surprised he hadn't drawn the connection before between the two. For what adventure could be greater than the great beyond.

"The great beyond left the woman with three things. A memento," Her hand brushed the scar, "The remnants of an old fisherman's boat," He noted there was no reference made to the fisherman who'd owned it... he didn't like what that implied, "And the knowledge that no matter how much she might yearn for what lay beyond these shores, they did not yearn for her. For not all voices that we hear call to *us*. She was unwelcome there and had been spared only as a favour to an old friend." She smiled sadly at Arthur, reaching out to give his hand a quick squeeze, "This is not my adventure little brother, it's yours."

And in many ways, for the first time, Arthur felt like he truly understood her. Neither at home here nor welcome there, trapped at the border of the beyond... And his heart broke for her, but not in a way that would allow him to stay. And based on the look in her eyes, she knew it.

"I'll miss you Mor."

"Actually, I think I'll miss *you* the most." She pulled him across the sand into another tight hug, "My brother." And somewhere in his heart, he knew her words were true.

"I'll come back." Morgana shook her head, pulling them both to their feet.

"You can't." And somehow, he knew that was truer still. "Be safe, or if you can't be, make those responsible regret it." Her eyes were fierce as she pressed something into his hands. He nodded. Her gaze remained that way, sharp as a blade, even as he boarded the vessel and pushed out to sea.

MORGANA HAD BEEN RIGHT. HE'D LOST TRACK of the east quite early into his travels, not a surprise given his lack of nautical experience, and yet... the waves seemed to part before him, urging him on, somewhere.

He would attribute it to the voice, but it had been oddly silent since he'd left the shores of his home. He hoped that silence bore no omen of things to come.

Settling back in the boat, Arthur distracted himself with the food he'd packed, his gaze catching on a second bundle as he tore into the slightly stale bread he'd managed to pilfer from the kitchen at home (they would likely miss it as much as they missed him, which was not a lot). It was Morgana's bundle, the one she'd handed to him on the beach. Something about it felt important. He hadn't been able to make out much about it from inside the wrappings. Only that it felt narrow and sturdy. A weapon perhaps? But what cause would he have for one of those?

Curiosity overpowering his hunger for the moment, he set the bread aside, wiping away any errant crumbs before carefully, almost reverently, unwrapping the gift his sister had given him.

The item inside had clearly been handcrafted from one of the island's hawthorn trees, but that was where his familiarity with the item he'd been gifted ended. He noted the shape of the thing. Long, pointed and surprisingly sharp. He noted this last discovery as he attempted to lift the item from its wrappings by the pointed end, resolving to take better care in future as he quickly set it back inside its wrappings.

Definitely a weapon of some sort then... but why not a knife or another more traditional weapon? Their isle proudly boasted the finest bladesmiths after all (not that they drew any point of comparison with the rest of the world), so why not one of those if she wanted him armed? And why a weapon at all? Morgana's tale, as informative as it was of her decision to stay, had left little room for deciphering much else from it. What was this weapon meant for? The threat that had driven her home? And if it was, would he really fare better than she had on her own doomed voyage?

He searched the folds of the cloth, hoping that their depths would reveal some hidden explanation for Morgana's gift. Instead, he unearthed a note, penned in his sister's hand.

'In case you do not yearn for that which yearns for you.'

Arthur carefully pocketed the note before settling the bundle aside. The weapon's use was meant for the voice then? A part of Arthur strongly rebelled at the thought. All the same, the weapon may still be useful to carry as a form of protection against other unfamiliar threats. And the note held a different value. Despite his inability to fully decipher her words, they were still *hers*. And if she was right, and he could never return to the isle, this might be the only piece of her he ever got to see again. He vowed to cherish it.

"You're still on this journey with me Mor. I'll find those answers for both of us." It made him feel a little silly to speak to what was essentially the open ocean, yet he couldn't help but feel he'd been heard. Though whether he was heard by Morgana, the voice or someone else entirely, he couldn't say.

ARTHUR HAD INTENDED TO MEMORISE EVERY detail of his arrival, from the first sight of new land to the pebbles and grains of sand that made up those foreign shores. It was his first look at the world beyond his home and he didn't want to miss a single detail.

Instead, Arthur suddenly awoke to find he'd already drifted to shore. And for a bleary-eyed moment or two he feared the tides had guided him back to the isle. But the towering walls of stone jutting from the ocean were a far cry from the pebbles and Hawthorn he was used to. They towered above the waves, demanding to be observed. They seemed unnatural, imposing, a barrier to the beyond... or to the before. After all, it was Arthur's home they now obscured. Or the home that had once been Arthur's...

A sudden rough hand against his shoulder had Arthur launching himself to the opposite side of the boat and away from the stranger who owned it. Because that was what this man was, the first man he'd ever met whom he could consider a *stranger*. What a novelty. Despite his misgivings, Arthur found himself leaning forward to inspect him a little closer.

This strange man reminded him of the elders, with the harsh lines of many years carved against his temple, yet the glimmer of concern in his eyes? That bore more similarity to Morgana than to them. Perhaps it was that which allowed him to accept the man's offered hand. The stranger's grip was surprisingly firm as he helped pull Arthur to his feet.

"You're not from these parts." It wasn't a question, yet the certainty of the statement surprised him. "We don't get many new faces around here lad, and I know all the faces on these docks. You're not from here..." His attention turned from Arthur to his boat, eyes widening a little at the inscription on the side. "*Definitely* not from around here." The boat bore little besides the name of his island and yet... This man seemed to *know* it at a glance.

"You know Avalon."

The man's concern quickly transformed to blind panic, his arms flapping about in a way that reminded Arthur a little of the seabirds he'd often observed on the shores of his isle. His bemusement must have shown because the man ceased his flapping in favour of shushing Arthur in a calmer but still slightly frenzied manner. A firm hand then proceeded to pull Arthur along the sands, a little further from the other boats he could now see gathered by the shores. It made Arthur wary... what was so bad about speaking the name of the isle he was raised on?

"Ears everywhere... I know of that place, aye. And if you have any sense at all, you will not allow anyone else to know of it, or at least to know that *you* know of it." Arthur's confusion must've shown on his face because the man added, "You aren't the first fisherman to wash up on our shores, but you would be the first to leave them." *Not the first?*

"There were more?"

"Aye lad, many more. Gone the moment they breathed that name to anyone who would listen. Bad things happen to those who come here from the isle..." Perhaps for the first time since leaving, Arthur felt the gravity of the situation settle in. Here he was, surrounded by strangers, some of which seemed to want to cause him real harm, and with no true idea of which was which.

"...I'm not from the isle," he eventually responded. It was an unconvincing lie, he knew, but it seemed to reassure the man.

"Good. Keep to that story lad. It's the only thing that'll protect you here." With that, the man left him, allowing Arthur to quickly gather his supplies, and his nerve, before exiting the boat. The sooner he got away from its tell-tale inscription, the better.

He would be fine. He would simply have to keep his head low until he found the means to leave this town. Blend in. He could do that. He'd been keeping out of the way of his parents and most of the island for *years*. He could do this.

HE COULD *NOT* DO THIS.

A few moments spent in the nearest tavern he'd found confirmed as much. From the moment he'd crossed the threshold, he'd felt eyes on him. From the patrons, the barkeep, *everyone*. They knew he was an outsider, that much was clear.

As long as they don't know what kind of outsider...

He quickly shuffled his way to an empty table, keeping his head down, quite literally, and hoping the room's attention would shift elsewhere.

It was clearly a fool's hope since, moments later, approaching footsteps and the slight jolt of the bench opposite him informed him he had company.

"Well, you're new."

"So I've been told." The stranger laughed at that, the sound a warm, hearty thing.

"I'm sure you have. The people of this town are many things, but subtle has never been one of them." Arthur looked up to meet the twinkling gaze of the man sitting opposite him, "My apologies on their behalf."

"It's fine... I mean, they aren't wrong."

"True enough. If it's any consolation, they were much the same with me when I arrived here." Arthur's surprise must have shown because the man's laughter returned, "Yes, I was the outsider once too. The good news is, eventually they adapt to your newness. You'll be one of us too, before you know it." Even though Arthur knew nothing of the man, including his name, he couldn't help but believe him. Or at least, believe that *he* believed his words.

"You think so?" The stranger nodded.

"Something tells me you belong here... That you're *exactly* where you're meant to be." They shared a smile at that. "I'm Waine, i not y, and yes, I know that's confusing. My parents were... eccentric people."

"It suits you." It did. In fact, something about that name rang familiar, yet not quite. "Mine's not as exciting."

"I wouldn't worry about that. I'm not the type to judge my company based on the title they bear."

"It's not a bad name, just not as unique as yours."

"Be grateful for that blessing." Arthur laughed.

"Arthur. My name's Arthur." He hadn't been aware he'd been speaking that loud, but he must've been, for the second those words left his lips, the room fell silent. He could feel eyes on him. The patrons, the barkeep, but Waine's were the ones he chose to observe. There was something in his gaze, something he couldn't quite place.

"I think you'd be surprised Arthur, how exciting that name might be…" Then the glimmer of whatever it was in the man's eyes was gone. "My apologies for this lot." He gestured to the room around him.

At his gesture, the room suddenly turned back to their conversations, almost pointedly ignoring the pair now. Arthur was unsure what to make of it.

"Why did they all-"

"An old story. More superstition really. But the folks here believe it."

"A story?" Waine nodded. "About what?"

"The Knights of Night."

"Centuries ago, in a time before the world we know came to be, there was a great kingdom, just moments away from these very shores. A kingdom of peace, prosperity, and honour, above all else. A kingdom ruled by a great King and his valiant Queen. And this kingdom was known as Camelot.

"It was said in its finest hour, even the ocean turned to precious gems to emulate the glory of its rulers. They were kind, benevolent and wise and their brave leadership drew many to these lands. Amongst those who journeyed there were ten men, whose destinies guided them to their future knighthoods. They became the King's most trusted subjects, his most loyal followers. The Knights of Camelot. And they loved him. Would gladly die for him. The King knew that and, despite his title, would do the same for them.

"For a while, Camelot thrived. Its monarchs wise, its people great, and its advisors unparalleled. It is said, the King even had one in his employ who could wield magic. *True* sorcery. Powerful enough to rule themselves, yet they too knelt to this great King. For they could see greater value in following this man than in ruling in his stead, so great was his leadership.

"But even the greatest dynasties fall. The great King fell one day in battle, with only his enemies to bear witness, and with him, Camelot fell too. His Knights first grew mournful, then bitter. Their mighty leader had been slain, and all in service and protection of them. They did not feel worthy of that sacrifice.

"As the years began to pass, the Knights withdrew from the world, seeking out only each other's company, and the company of others who had suffered this great loss. They removed themselves from their remnants of their beloved monarch's world, and in doing so, found another."

"Another?" Waine laughed.

"I speak of forgotten kingdoms and magic, yet this is the first detail you question?"

"Kingdoms are forgotten all the time."

"And magic?" Arthur shrugged, not entirely sure he wanted to discuss the voice with this stranger and *certain* that telling him of his suspiciously easy travel from the island to this town was unwise. As nice as this man seemed, the old man's warning still lingered in his mind. *Bad things happen to those who come here from the isle...*

"Well, this other world was not entirely new. An old friend of these Knights offered them a choice, to live as they were, miserable and dejected, or to cast off these sorrows and be reborn. It was an easy choice. The

Knights cast away what was left of their former selves and became something new."

"What did they become?" Waine smiled.

"Depends on who you ask. Some say they drifted apart, travelled to different kingdoms, and found meaning there. Some say their attempts failed and they were lost, both to grief and to time. And some... some say that they truly were reborn as something new. Something-"

"Terrible." Arthur jumped at the gruff voice from the table next to theirs. "They became abominations. Monsters."

"I don't remember asking for your input." Waine's tone was curt, his gaze sharp and cold in a way that almost made Arthur want to grab for the weapon Morgana had gifted him... Not that he'd have a clue how to use it.

"You were telling the story wrong. Kid has a right to know *all* of it." Without hesitation, the man got up from his own bench, taking a seat next to Arthur. "There's a reason they're called the Knights of Night. Because day itself shuns these beasts. They cannot exist beneath the sun, but at night? They reveal their true monstrosity."

"What *kind* of monstrosity?" Arthur looked away from Waine. The dark look in the man's eyes had him shuffling closer to the new arrival at their table, even though that look didn't appear to be trained on him.

"They long since sacrificed their own humanity so now they prey on the humanity of others. Sometimes killing them-" The man pressed two of his fingers against Arthur's wrist, "Always leaving their mark behind." He suddenly recalled Morgana's scars and shuddered. Both men seemed to pick up on it. "Never trust a man you cannot see in the day, that's the only way to truly know you're safe."

"*Thank you* for your *contribution*. I'm sure your table is missing you." The stranger seemed to ignore Waine, placing a hand on Arthur's shoulder.

"Remember, always look to the sun. Its light will reveal all truths concealed away in the dark." Arthur nodded, watching with lingering unease as the man made his way back to his original table, leaving him alone with Waine in an awkward silence.

"Again, I feel I must apologise for Abe. He feels very *passionately* about certain tales these folks tell."

"Are they true?"

"The tales?" Arthur forced himself to meet Waine's gaze, finding the same warmth and softness he had seen there before... He found it more difficult to trust it now he'd seen how cold the man could be.

"Depends on who you ask. But the folks here definitely think so."

"And the deaths?"

"All small towns have *something* they blame for people dying. Ours just happens to be a group of ancient knights." That at least Arthur could believe. He forced himself to relax. There could be any number of reasons for the tension he'd just witnessed between Waine and 'Abe'. It didn't mean either man was truly dangerous. Did it?

"But how do these ancient knights relate to my name?" He finally asked, remembering the reason for Waine's tale.

"Well, the reason these Knights had to accept the offer of a new life varies, but there's one in particular that recurs the most. The promise that, with enough patience, their great leader would one day return. And when he does, his Knights would be waiting for him... They call it the prophecy of *The Once and Future King*. And that King's name, if legends are to be believed, was Arthur."

A Once and Future King... How was that even possible? Surely if the King had died that ruled out the possibility of any future ruling. And why would *his* name bear any significance to that anyway. He could hardly be the only Arthur here. He certainly hadn't been on the isle.

"So, they took notice because I reminded them of a prophecy?"

"That and you're the first man bearing that name to pass through this town in about five hundred years."

"But Arthur's a common name-"

"Not here." Waine rolled his eyes at the input from Abe, who was making no secret of continuing to monitor their conversation. "Legends say bad things happen to people with that name in this town. It's considered cursed."

"Cursed?" Arthur's sense of alarm flared up stronger than ever, "How is it cursed?"

"It is *not* cursed, and neither are you." Waine assured him, his tone a little harsher than he likely intended for it to be. "These are just superstitions, nothing more."

Abe looked ready to respond to that, but someone else at the table with him shook his head, glancing warily at both Waine and Arthur. Arthur wasn't sure how *he* was worthy of that stare. He was about as threatening as a baby seal. Still, whatever silent warning Abe's companion had offered, he seemed to heed it, turning away from the pair.

"It is good to meet you, Arthur. And if any of these superstitions turn out to bear some truth, know that you will have me to protect you. I won't let any harm come to you here. I swear it." Arthur wanted to believe him, but there was something about the patron's looks, about Abe's words, that made him question that vow. Because how could Arthur dismiss curses and prophecies when he'd decided to travel the world on the whims of a voice only he could hear? Either he was mad, or the world really *could* be filled with monsters... and if either was true, could Waine really protect him from them?

ARTHUR COULDN'T REMEMBER FALLING asleep when he'd turned in for the night, but he must've since the shabby furnishings of the room he'd rented faded, leaving in their place something familiar, yet not. Ancient, ornate... Like the rooms *he* would have slept in. The *other* Arthur.

Arthur.

The voice! It was as if he'd summoned it by thinking of him. This great King... was *he* who the voice had been calling to all this time? Had it never been Arthur it had wanted at all?

Arthur.

The voice grew louder. And clearer. For the first time he could discern little nuances in its tone. It sounded pleased, but a quiet sort of pleased, as if still lying in wait for some greater pleasure to come.

Hello?

Abruptly the voice fell silent. In fact, all sound disappeared entirely, in the way it only truly can in a dream. Then, just as sudden, a shadowy figure appeared at the foot of the bed. Arthur couldn't make out its features, only a blurred outline, and yet... Arthur knew with a certainty that *this* was the voice that had called to him all these years.

You hear me.

It wasn't a question.

Can you see me?

He was uncertain how to respond. He could see *something* but... Was this really how the voice looked?

No matter if you can't... I can see you. Arthur.

A shrill noise drew Arthur from the conversation, ancient drapes melting away to sparse furnishings as a loud repetitive thudding sounded at the door. It burst open before Arthur had a chance to answer, a grim looking barmaid entering at haste. Her narrow eyes peered closely at him before she nodded quietly to herself.

"You need to leave."

"It's barely dawn! I can't just-"

"Abe is dead." It took Arthur a moment to realise who she meant, but when he did... he felt a sudden chill creep along his spine. Like a caress, so tangible he almost turned to seek out a third party in the room.

"What does that have to do with-"

"Abe's dead and everyone saw you talking. To him and to the outsider."

"Outsider?"

"I always said Lucy was wrong about him. Ever since he arrived, there's been far too many folks who've-"

"Since who arrived?"

"Your friend at the bar." *Waine.* Arthur felt his stomach turn. The man had offered him shelter for the night, so he wouldn't have to use his limited funds on a room at the inn... what would've happened if he'd taken him up on it?

"You're sure it was him?"

The woman's gaze softened a little as she nodded. "No one else had the opportunity to do it, 'cept for you, and something tells me you don't have the stomach for it." Given the way it was currently churning, Arthur couldn't help but agree. "That won't stop the others from coming for you though. Abe was eccentric, but he's one of us... And they heard your name. There'll be plenty of folks who'll lump the pair of you together in this... no matter how misplaced their blame seems to be." Arthur didn't even realise he was shaking until a warm but firm hand landed on his shoulder, "It's not your fault you're cursed lad, but you need to go before folks around here decide to blame you anyway."

It suddenly struck Arthur that this woman was attempting to be kind. It was this, combined with the fear of who Waine might target next, that spurred him into motion. Travelling light had its advantages. He had few belongings to begin with, and those he did were mostly packed. With the woman's assistance, he made quick work of the rest, with only Harker's vial attempting to escape the confines of his belongings. The woman's gaze turned oddly sharp as she spotted it.

"Aqua Benedicta."

'...I'm sorry?"

"No need to apologise."

"No, I didn't mean-" His response was quickly cut off when the woman promptly uncapped the bottle and doused him in its contents. "What was that for?"

"You'll thank me later." Somehow Arthur doubted it. Yet he hardly had the luxury of questioning his saviour any further as they fled the room, heading down a side alley to where a horse and a harried looking man stood waiting.

"Leave now and you should get out unseen. If they assume you didn't stay the night, chances are they'll blame the Knights and leave you out of it."

"The Knights did this? I thought Waine had-" Something in the man's gaze told Arthur he would receive no further explanations, so he set his questions aside, allowing the gruff man to help him onto his steed.

"Ride west until you see an inn bearing the sign of the dragon. The folks there will take you in."

"...What's a dragon?" The pair exchanged a look before the woman quickly rolled up her sleeve, revealing something red and scaled against the ochre of her skin.

"That's a dragon lad. It'll be like that, but bigger."

A loud clang and the sound of racing footsteps cut off any response Arthur might've had. The woman quickly tugged down her sleeve as the man urged him forward.

"Go!" Arthur awaited no further instruction. With only the vaguest directions, he set off, hoping that he'd somehow know his destination when he found it.

As he rode from the city, he could feel eyes on him. Seemingly from everywhere. He hoped they were friendly, or at the very least indifferent. And he sincerely hoped that Waine was not among them.

I won't let any harm come to you here.

If this was Waine's version of protection, Arthur didn't want it.

He wondered if Abe had known, when he'd spoken to Arthur that night, that it would lead to this... Was this his fault? The woman had assured him otherwise and yet, Waine had only seemed angry with Abe when he'd intervened in the story about the Knights. What was it Abe had told Arthur?

At night they reveal their true monstrosity. Never trust a man you cannot see in the day.

Well, he'd certainly been right about the monstrous part, Arthur just had to hope he'd been right about the rest, and that the rising sun would protect him as he travelled to the dragon-marked inn. The rest he would have to leave in the hands of the strangers who awaited him there.

As he fled past the town's borders, amidst the cantering of hooves, Arthur heard the voice return.

Arthur.

But its tone had changed. Before it had been pleased, anticipatory. Now? It sounded *angry.* For the first time since he'd started to hear it, Arthur ignored the voice and continued to ride.

～

SURPRISINGLY, ARTHUR ARRIVED AT THE INN he'd been instructed to with relative ease, give or take a sudden dark storm rolling in, moments after he'd fled the village, and some ominous howling. Wolves, his mind had supplied, though from where he couldn't be certain. The isle had rarely spoken of the world beyond its shores, and the creatures were as unfamiliar to him as the rest of this strange and treacherous land.

Finally, just as the faintest glimmers of twilight began to creep in amidst the clouds, he arrived at a building marked with a bright red dragon... Or at least a bright red *something* that vaguely resembled the design he'd seen on the woman's arm. Despite the lingering rain, Arthur found himself admiring the details of the beast as he drew closer. Something in the scales and the fire of this noble creature seemed familiar too. He dismounted his steed, lightly rapping on the door. His knuckles had barely touched the wood when he was suddenly swept inside and drawn into a tight, warm hug.

"It's you!"

"...I guess?" The man drew back.

"Of course, sorry I just... we'd heard there was an Arthur. I guess I didn't really expect it to be, well, *you*."

"...Sorry to disappoint-"

"Not a disappointment-"

"-but I don't think I'm who you think I am."

"You're Arthur of Avalon." The joviality was gone, so quickly that Arthur had to question if it had ever existed to begin with, "You're exactly who I think you are... For which, I can only apologise."

"Apologise? For what?"

"For who you are. Since who you are means that, now you've left the isle, you'll never truly be safe."

"Safe from what?"

"From *them*." Arthur had a feeling he knew what the man referred to and yet, it was superstition, wasn't it? Waine had certainly claimed as much. *But Waine clearly couldn't be trusted. After all, last time he'd trusted that man, another had wound up dead. Abe was dead. And he had believed otherwise... He had mentioned monsters and curses and prophecies... But maybe he'd been wrong. Maybe Waine was a monster simply because he was a murderer. It wasn't as if Arthur had ever seen him refuse to walk into the sun. It didn't mean he was one of the... Night Knights? Was that what he'd called them? Not important. The point was, the threat Arthur was fleeing had been a human murderer and superstition, right?*

"They're a story. A-"

"Very real threat that has decimated villages across this coastline, all in one name." The man set a firm hand on Arthur's shoulders. He did his best not to flinch under its grip, "Yours."

"I never asked them to."

"We know... No one would ask for this."

"For what? And who's we?"

"Those are the questions, aren't they? What makes the Knights what they are? How is it they wait for you?" The man drew back his sleeve, revealing a litter of scattered marks, just like Morgana's, criss-crossed in jagged patterns. "I know not how they came to be, but I know what they are and that they *must* cease to plague us. They are an infection, Pendragon... As for the we, I may only be so bold as to offer my own name. Mordred."

"Pendragon?"

"Your name. Your *real* name."

"My name is Arthur."

"Arthur Pendragon, yes. The once and-"

"I'm nobody's king."

The man scoffed. "*You* might not be, but *you-you* definitely was."

"Me-me?"

"Original you!"

"I *am* original me?" Arthur hated that his words sounded like a question.

"None of us are truly original Arthur. To be fair, the 'original' you was likely a copy too, just a copy that a certain kind of monster happened to take a liking to a little *too* much... hence non-original you being in danger now."

"...Was any of that supposed to make sense?"

The man sighed, kicking a stool in Arthur's direction which he moved to dodge before recognising it for the offer, and not attack, that it was. He tentatively took a seat.

"Many years ago, there was a Great King. I assume someone filled you in on *that* much." Arthur nodded, "Good, saves me time. Well, him and a lot of others died in a great battle towards the end of his reign, but not all of them. The Knights, the Magician and the Queen escaped, both the battle and death itself. Everyone else. Dead. Deceased. Returned to the cycle."

"The cycle?"

"It's where all of us go when we pass. Complete our journey, return to the cycle, be born anew. The timings vary, not an exact science but... sooner or later, we all come back. And you did come back. Great King Arthur."

"So... you really think I'm some long dead King?"

"No. I think you're what comes after greatness."

"I'm not sure if I should be relieved or offended." Arthur attempted a laugh, but it fell flat.

"Neither. It's not an insult, and it won't keep you safe from them."

"Who are *they?*"

"His court. The ones that got left behind."

"But... how did they get left behind if everyone returns to the 'cycle'."

"The Magician stopped the wheel." Arthur stared at him, uncomprehendingly.

"Is everyone who doesn't live on the isle deliberately vague?"

"You expect me to believe Avalon told you more than I have?"

"Well... they mostly avoided the subject of anything beyond the isle actually." The man snorted.

"Typical Avalon... Bet she *hates* it there."

"She?" The man either didn't hear him or pretended not to hear.

"The Magician extended their lives, but at a cost. The Court lives in name only. Truly, they died with their King in that battle."

"And the Queen?"

"Dead too, in every way that matters at least. And in her wake more death follows, weaponizing her curse against the world now barred to her." The man bared his teeth as if to emphasise his point, in a manner that should've been comical. Arthur wasn't laughing.

"And the magician?"

"Exists as he always has, which is to say he has *always* courted death. He may even be death himself."

"...What do they want with me?" Mordred sighed as he moved to the window, frowning at the dusk as it claimed the landscape beyond it.

"They want *you*. They want the echo of what they once had. Their once and future King... I'm glad they sent you to me before the court could find you. I won't let them spread their curse to you, I swear it."

"You'll protect me from them?"

"In the only way I can." The man was suddenly across the room. His arms drew tight around Arthur, one across his chest whilst the other pressed against his throat. Arthur wheezed, struggling frantically against the man's immovable frame, "I am truly sorry, but this is the only kindness I know how to grant. It will be over soon, *Ewythr*."

And perhaps Mordred was right for Arthur remembered little else before the dark surged up and swallowed him whole.

It was perhaps a surprise then when Arthur awoke, some amount of time later, with a thudding head and a raspy throat... surprising because he awoke at all. And maybe a little because of the soft mattress he woke up on.

At the end of it sat an elegant man, dressed in robes that seemed to hold the secrets of the stars within their folds. He was perched in a way that reminded Arthur an awful lot of the seabirds he sometimes watched back on the isle. The way they would lie in wait, carefully assessing their prey, in total stillness... until they finally struck. It was an unsettling comparison to draw, especially when this stranger was watching him so intently.

"Hello Arthur." *The voice.* "I can only apologise for how we met. I would have much preferred talking to you in a more casual setting, but when Waine informed me of your flight, I suspected the worst, and it appears I was right." Arthur felt oddly chastised, despite having never met the man before him.

"I'm sorry?" Or at least, those were the words he attempted to voice. The hoarseness of his throat obscured the words, though the man before him appeared to understand them well enough.

"No matter. What is done is dealt with." Arthur was caught a little off guard by the statement, the coldness of it. He had... never heard the voice like this before.

"Mordred?"

"Decided it would be better to allow us to catch up, rather than interfere any further. I've been assured Waine is taking *very* good care of him." His body gave an almost reflexive shudder at the thought.

"So, he's-"

"As dead as he intended for you to be. Yes. Shouldn't have spent so long catching up with family I suppose." The shock of Mordred's actions seemed to finally hit with those words. It had been so sudden, so intense, so completely without warning and...

"Family?"

"Your nephew. Really took after his mother. As sharp of a thorn in my side as she always was."

"I don't have any siblings."

The man's answering smirk was sharp enough to carve through steel. "Not in this life, Arthur."

What was that supposed to mean? He'd only lived one life, despite what everyone seemed to think. He'd been born an only child. He *knew* that... but he'd always felt that Morgana was...

"-like a sister?" Arthur recoiled as the voice-turned-man easily finished his thoughts. "She was, once. Before she lost that right."

"Lost that right? How can someone lose the right to be family?"

"By stealing you away from all that you loved." The man shifted closer to him, "by stealing you from *me*."

"I'm not yours."

The man smiled serenely. "You were. In another life. You will be." Arthur narrowly repressed the urge to scream.

"I'm not who you think I-"

"I think you're the little boy who heard me. Who has *always* heard me. The one who grew into the man who sought me out. *My* Arthur." A cold chill hung in the air between them.

"I'm *not* yours."

"You aren't?" The man titled his head, catlike. "You come when you're called, don't you? Despite your loving family, your sister and all you know and love existing on the island you left, on Avalon, you came. Because *I* asked."

"I came because I was curious."

"About *me*. You were drawn to me, Arthur. And you still are." Arthur belatedly realised he'd been leaning towards the man and frantically pulled back. The man's answering smirk was difficult to behold so he looked elsewhere, catching sight of the bundles he travelled with, at the side of the bed. Just within reach.

"You hold no power over me." Arthur met the man's gaze, defiant, and doing his best not to shrink under its intensity. In that moment he knew what it was to truly be prey. For *this* was a predator in action and Arthur was simply... holding his gaze so the man wouldn't look elsewhere and realize the weapon Arthur was pulling from his belt.

"Don't I? You still feel it, don't you? The call? The voice?" Arthur's hands readied the weapon, finally averting his gaze. "I *know* you do." A surprisingly warm hand cupped his cheek, forcing their eyes to meet again, "Did you know, you called back? Not just when you left Avalon. You have *always* called to me, my Arthur."

"I'm not *yours*."

"*You are.*" The words were hard. Deliberate. "And I will *always* answer your call." Arthur's hand arched up, pointed weapon in hand. The man didn't even flinch as his other hand grasped Arthur's forcing it to go limp and drop the one defence Morgana had gifted him. "First the holy water, now this? *Clever boy.* Though perhaps a little smarter if you hadn't telegraphed your intentions quite so clearly... A gift from your sister, no doubt. A shame to waste it on me."

"There's no one else to waste it on."

"So, you admit it's a waste? If it's any consolation, your other little trick left its mark... on Waine at least. It's what he deserves for letting you slip away from him, wouldn't you say?"

Arthur grit his teeth, refusing to grant him a response.

"Don't do that Arthur. I've waited so long to hear you call for me. *Truly* call."

"I'm not calling anymore." The man laughed, the sound a cold parody of humour.

"You believe that... But right now, you're all but screaming-"

"In fear-"

"*Never.* I bear no threat to you." The hand which had disarmed him now moved to Arthur's chest, "This part of you knows it. I am a threat to all, but *never* to you."

"Then what are you?"

"Your advisor. Your friend. *Yours.*" And somehow, in that moment, Arthur heard one last whisper from the voice. A name. *His* name.

"Merlin." The man's answering smile tore through the dark like lightning.

"My King."

ARTHUR COULDN'T HELP BUT BE HYPER-AWARE of Waine's presence amidst the Knights gathered to bear witness. The man looked relieved to see him, and perhaps a little guilty. Something told Arthur that guilt had more to do with his close encounter with Mordred than Waine's role in Abe's death... He instinctively shuffled closer to Merlin, even though he suspected the man-magician-creature had far more blood on his hands... At least Arthur hadn't known those people. At least he didn't have to look into his eyes and know the faces of the men he'd killed for him. At least *he* didn't make him feel complicit in those deaths.

Beside Waine, a pair of unnaturally beautiful individuals stood. The taller, a man, bowed his head as Arthur passed, his hand entwined with his radiant companion. She burned with the sharpness of a distant star, pale and perfect, and Arthur knew at a glance that this was once Arthur's Queen.

Yours no longer.

Arthur had to agree with the voice. This woman had never been his. And the other Arthur, long dead, held no claim over who she was now. He could see that the years without the former King had driven her heart elsewhere and he found he was glad of it. Perhaps because of who he wasn't? Or was?

You are him.

Arthur wasn't so sure.

My Arthur, my King.

That at least he believed.

He reached the end of the procession, allowing firm but gentle hands to guide him towards a dais with an ornate looking chair in the centre. After a moment's hesitation, he sat, doing his best to ignore the strange impression he had of walking in the shadow of greatness and falling short. There was no doubting, after all, that this was *his* seat, *his* throne.

"Yours." Merlin murmured, "all of this is yours."

The intensity of the room seemed to sharpen as Merlin suddenly drew closer, kneeling before Arthur in a moment of supplication that, to Arthur at least, only seemed to strengthen the revelation that it was not him who held the *true* power here.

"*I* am yours." It was both true and not true, "and you are mine. *My* King."

Arthur deliberately looked ahead as Merlin took his wrist in hand, turning away from this predator of predators. *His monster*. He felt something that might have been a smile against his wrist.

He was suddenly reminded of a moment when he

was a little boy. The first time he'd seen a fish get caught. He'd been spying on the trainee fishermen, inspired to one day follow in their footsteps if it gave him a chance to see beyond Avalon's shores. He'd watched as one of the trainees caught a fish. Watched it struggle before slowly, sadly, settling into a quiet acceptance. Arthur had sworn that day that if he ever was caught like that fish, he wouldn't give in so easily. He'd fight until his captors stood down and set him free.

As it turned out, he was wrong.

Sharp pain tore through his wrist as dual blades sunk home. Merlin's gift. His curse. It *burned*. In a moment he saw it all. Morgana, the isle, Waine, Abe, Mordred, Merlin, *him*. A man stood at the edge of the room. Tall, regal, Kinglike despite the fact that he wore Arthur's skin. A ghost.

I am not him.

The ghost smiled.

You will be.

Arthur fell. The Great King rose to take his place.

It is important to remember, before we go chasing the adventures we are called to, that not all of the voices we hear call to *us*. Sometimes they call to many. To others. To anyone. Sometimes to someone similar. Or forgotten. To an echo of before. They cry out to an ideal, a memory. Not to us.

And even when those whispers are for us, and us alone, sometimes it is still better to heed the warning of Avalon's pale lady, and not answer.

For not all voices that call to us have the intention of giving us back once we're done with our adventure.

The House Spider

TAYLOR MCLEOD

O nce upon a time there lived a little girl who hated spiders. She did not fear them, as most little girls do, but rather she hated that they existed. Little Lucy loved all things pretty, and fluffy, and cute. Spiders were very seldom any of these things. Little Lucy therefore hated all spiders, and she took it upon herself to rid her world from them whenever the opportunity arose.

Little Lucy was always taught by her parents to never kill a spider, another thing that Little Lucy hated. Mummy and Daddy would ensure that if Little Lucy ever found a spider that they would be the ones to gently catch them in a glass and then place them outside to find a new home to live in.

"Spiders are important little animals." Daddy

explained to Little Lucy one day as he gently removed a cellar spider from underneath the sink. "They make sure no other nasty bugs get into the house and help keep the house clean and tidy."

Little Lucy had scoffed at this idea. How could something so ugly, and so creepy and something with so many legs, be able to keep a house clean? So as far as Little Lucy was concerned, all spiders needed to die. Preferably in a horrible manner to reflect how horrible looking spiders always were.

Little Lucy learnt very quickly that if she saw a spider, she was the only one who could properly deal with it. She once found a garden spider that had found its way into the family bathroom. The little spider had been trying to climb up the outside of the house so that it could find a suitable place to build its nest, but had gotten confused by the big open window. Little Lucy had been watching as the little spider crawled through the open window, down along the counter top and had then slipped into the bathroom sink when the porcelain was too smooth and shiny for the spider's feet to grip onto. She had then flushed the trespassing creep down the drain.

This was how Little Lucy dealt with most spiders. She assumed the spiders were drawn to the bathroom because of the amount of shiny white surfaces that must have shone in the sunlight everyday. This was where she found the majority of her spider enemies and she dealt with them in very much the same way as she had dealt with that annoying garden spider in the sink. She would watch them all get sucked down into the drain, knowing that she was keeping her house clean and her family safe. Mummy and Daddy didn't seem to know about this silent act that Little Lucy did for them, for they never once thanked her or asked how she could be so brave as to deal with such grotesque monsters so regularly. They would just look disappointed, which just made Little Lucy even more angry.

But that was not until Little Lucy went into the attic one day with Mummy. Mummy liked to paint and Mummy was actually incredibly gifted at painting. She would paint beautiful landscapes of rolling hills, snow capped mountains or tropical beaches. She would paint dancers in movement or lovers in a warm embrace in the rain. She would paint with colours that Little Lucy could not even name and each painting seemed to awaken emotions in Little Lucy that she would never experience organically. But painting was also very messy work.

Mummy and Daddy had bought the family home when Little Lucy was still Baby Lucy. The attic space was well insulated but the previous owners had used the space as a dumping ground for the things that did not have a place down with the rest of the house. Unfortunately Mummy and Daddy had been using the space in the same manner. However, last Christmas Daddy had gifted Mummy with a brand new easel and some sparkly new paints for her to play with. They had put the easel and the paints in the attic while they tried to find space for it all downstairs, before they both came to the realisation that they could use the attic as Mummy's work space.

"Now be careful with some of these boxes." Mummy had said to Little Lucy as she handed her a small box of paints. "Let's move all of the paints to that side of the attic, and then we can figure out what to do with the rest of them."

It had taken Mummy, Daddy and Little Lucy nearly a month to fully clear, organise and decorate the attic to be a functioning work space. In the middle of the room sat Mummy's easel, with the paints all neatly stored next to it in an old chest of drawers that Mummy had painted to match the decor of the rest of the room. The attic was not very big, but it had a cosy and warm feel to it. Little Lucy loved to sit in the attic for hours with Mummy and watch her paint her exciting scenes. Sometimes Mummy would even let

Little Lucy help with the finishing touches of splashing colours across the painting or adding extra stars to the night sky.

That was until Steve arrived.

"Gordon!!" Mummy had screamed in a high pitch yelp one day. Daddy and Little Lucy raced up the stairs to the attic to find Mummy stood by her easel, clutching a paint brush to her chest and whimpering slightly as she stared intently at one corner of the attic.

"Maggie?!" Daddy asked in shock as he took Mummy in his arms and looked her up and down. "What's wrong? What's happened?"

"He's over there." She whimpered in a high pitched whisper. She pointed one paint stained hand in the direction she was staring and Daddy and Little Lucy followed her gaze.

Sitting motionless in the corner of the attic was the biggest spider that Little Lucy had ever seen. It was bigger than her hand. Possibly even bigger than Daddy's hand. Little Lucy even heard Daddy let out one of the bad words that she was told never to repeat as he caught sight of the huge spider before him. The spider had a thick, dark brown body and even from this distance Little Lucy could see the fuzzy texture of the hair that covered it. It had eight long legs that seemed to stretch out to fill the entire attic. These too were thick, dark brown and horrifically fuzzy. Little Lucy grimaced as she realised that she could see the knees and ankles of each of the spider's legs and she wanted to immediately snap them. The spider stared at the family, and the family stared back into the empty voids of the spider's eight black eyes.

"Oh he's a biggun." Daddy muttered under his breath. He shuffled on his feet slightly as he looked around him. "Yeah I think I'm going to need some Tupperware for this fella."

"Please hurry back." Mummy said with a scared laugh. "If it moves I think I might just cry."

"He's not going to hurt you. Just...don't chase him." Daddy gave Mummy a quick kiss on the forehead before turning to head back down to the kitchen. "Lucy sweetie, don't go near it." He muttered just before he left.

But Little Lucy was already preparing to sprint towards the beast and destroy it. How dare this creature come into her house. Into her Mummy's special room. How dare this beast fill such a pretty room with its ugliness. It needed to be taught a lesson. If Daddy captured it and released it into the garden, the disrespectful evil would simply climb back in. No one wanted it here and it needed to never come back. Little Lucy could hear Daddy crashing about downstairs trying to find a container big enough for this monster, but he would be too slow. What if the spider sensed weakness and tried to eat them both while they stood there waiting for Daddy to return? What if it tried to eat all of Mummy's paintings? What if it tried to invite all of its horrible little friends over and soon the entire attic was nothing more than a spider party house? Oh no, that was not happening. Little Lucy would die before she let a spider take over her home.

She tensed her legs as much as she could and before Mummy could stop her she ran full steam at the spider. But before she could even take a third step, the spider had vanished. There was a small squeak of horror from Mummy as the spider seemed to melt into the darkness behind it, and Little Lucy felt her blood pulse through her veins in anger as she frantically looked about her feet trying to spot where the spider had gone. Was it going to go for her legs first? Or perhaps try to attack from behind? She whirled around in a fit of rage as the spider disappeared before her eyes. She was so angry she began to cry.

"Oh sweetie," Mummy was now beside her. "Shush sweet girl, it's ok. The spider's just gone back home." She patted Little Lucy's head soothingly as she carried her out of the attic and downstairs to join Daddy.

"What happened?" Daddy looked up from the pile of Tupperware containers that were now strewn around his feet. He came to join Mummy in soothing Little Lucy but she was just too angry to be calmed.

"I think the sight of the spider just terrified her." Mummy said to Daddy as she began to gently rock Little Lucy in her arms the way she had done when Little Lucy was far smaller.

"Silly girly." Daddy muttered with a soft laugh. "The spider can't hurt you. He's gone now."

But Little Lucy was more annoyed that she could not hurt the spider. She hated that this thing was now somewhere in her home, watching and waiting.

It took most of the evening to calm Little Lucy down again, although deep down she was still furious at the spider. The absolute disrespect that spider had shown was the most insulted Little Lucy had ever felt. Even more insulted than when Toby had called her a 'stinky butthead' at school that one time. This spider was now the worst spider that had ever existed. And Little Lucy vowed to not rest until this spider was brought to justice and this evil was removed from her home.

Later that week, Little Lucy lay in bed, staring angrily up at her ceiling. She had tried several more times to catch and kill the monster spider, but the beast would disappear as quickly as he appeared, which only fuelled the fires of hatred within little Lucy. That stupid spider was mocking her and she hated him even more for it. Mummy and Daddy didn't understand her frustrations and just thought she was scared of him, but Little Lucy couldn't expect them to understand. They cared for spiders. They had even started to call the giant house spider 'Steve' as a sick nickname, like he was a pet that they were welcoming into the home. Mummy would even comment how Steve had joined her for a little bit of painting earlier in the day. Mummy and Daddy would laugh as Little Lucy felt her blood heat within her.

She rolled over in bed, pulling her teddy close to her and trying to remove Steve and his creepy crawly minions from her mind so that she could actually sleep. But then she noticed a faint shadow on the edge of her bed, moving slowly towards her, and she could feel the very faint movements across the top of her duvet as the shadow moved closer.

Without hesitating she rolled over and turned the lamp on her bedside table on. Sitting on the end of her bed, big eyes shining in the lamp light, was Steve.

"Get out of here!" Little Lucy said and went to throw her teddy at him. But the spider saw this and seemed to begin floating away, up towards the ceiling.

"I am not your enemy, little one." Steve appeared to be talking. Little Lucy could not see any movement from his fanged mouth, but could feel the words as they echoed around her head, as though he was speaking directly into her ear. She felt herself shudder at the thought of his spindly legs touching her. "I am here to protect this home."

"We don't need protection. That's what Mummy and Daddy do and I am here to help them. We don't need anyone else." Little Lucy replied back sharply.

"And you all do a very good job. But my warriors and I protect the house from The Others. From the creatures you really do not want in your house. From the creatures that could do serious damage to your home and to you and your parents." Steve responded. His voice was cool and calm as he hovered just above the bed, suspended from the ceiling by a thin line of silk.

"You are not wanted here!" Little Lucy raised her teddy again to throw it at him but Steve once again shimmied up his silk escape rope out of her reach.

"We are here to help you. I have sent one of my family to help in your garden, one to help in your bathroom and one to keep the pests out of the house entirely. They will help me protect this home and will make sure none of The Others get in. Please do not harm them. If you do, I will not be responsible for what happens to you or your family."

Little Lucy had heard enough and aimlessly threw her teddy towards where Steve was. The teddy flew through the air but came nowhere close to where Steve was still floating. But the act got her message across. Steve stared at her for a moment longer and then silently ascended his silk line and disappeared into the darkness of her room once more. Little Lucy did not have the time nor the patience to listen to his inane ramblings anymore. He was just a spider. What on earth could one spider really do to hurt her?

THE NEXT MORNING LITTLE LUCY AWOKE feeling hazy. She had barely managed to sleep, tossing and turning all night following Steve's stupid visit, but now she was awake she wondered if it had all just been a dream. Spiders did not talk and they certainly weren't protectors. She found Mummy in the kitchen making breakfast for everyone, and Daddy was outside in the garden tending to his flowers as he did most days. Mummy called out that breakfast was ready and the small family ate together as they also did most mornings.

"Maybe today you can help me in the garden?" Daddy suggested to Little Lucy once they had finished eating. Little Lucy nodded excitedly and followed Daddy outside into the crisp morning air.

Their garden was small but magnificent, all thanks to Daddy's very green thumb and hard work. There was a small patch of grass in the middle, just big enough to put a paddling pool in during the very hot summer months, and then a thick flower bed that ran along the garden fences. Summer was slowly drawing to a close, so many of Daddy's flowers were beginning to wilt. Daddy led Little Lucy over to his rose bush and was carefully explaining to her how to tend to the flowers, showing her which petals to remove from a wilting flower and which dead buds needed to be removed.

"Just in time it seems," Daddy said with a sigh and he pointed at an area of the rose bush that was covered in tiny orange specks. Little Lucy leaned in closer and realised that they were tiny little bugs, all climbing over one another as they made their way along the rose bush. "These little guys here are aphids. They are any gardener's worst nightmare. They eat everything and are clearly starting to make a meal of my rose bush."

"Should we get rid of them?" Little Lucy said, concerned that all of Daddy's hard work in the garden could be ruined by such a tiny bug.

"No, there are not very many of them. At least not enough to warrant us doing anything." Daddy said simply. "They'll disappear as the flowers start to fall off and will be gone once the weather gets colder. Now let me get you some special tools and we can start on the vegetables?"

Little Lucy watched as Daddy stood and headed back inside the house. She looked back at the little bugs as they rushed about on the stems of the roses. Then she looked higher up and saw a small garden spider hanging amongst the rose bush. They were perfectly still, hanging silently in the middle of their web which was built between two particularly thick rose stems. As Little Lucy watched, a few of the aphids found their way onto the spider's web and like lightning the garden spider pounced on them, biting them and then wrapping the bodies up with their thick webbing. The spider then returned to sit in the middle of their web and seemed to meet Little Lucy's gaze.

She could feel repulsion rising in her. She had flashbacks of what she had hoped was a dream, but was now beginning to realise that Steve really had been in her room last night. Little Lucy began to think that this was the spider that Steve had told her about, the spider that was supposedly going to help their family in the garden. Except...this spider was just a greedy, fat spider. Daddy had already explained that aphids were not a problem and that there was no need to harm them, yet here this spider was killing them and saving their bodies for later as though it was going to throw a massive aphid eating party for all of its horrible friends. This wasn't helping because the garden didn't even need the help. Daddy had everything under control, so who did this spider think it was to move into Daddy's carefully cared for garden just so it could gorge itself on little bugs. Steve had been wrong. The garden didn't need any help at all.

"Please don't harm me," The spider said to her gently. "Without me to keep their numbers down, they will overrun your garden. I will not go into any other part of the garden if that would make you happy, but if I die, so does your garden. Please...let me help. My King knows what is needed to keep The Others out."

"We don't want your help." Little Lucy responded bluntly. "Tell your King that none of you are welcome here."

"Please listen to us. Listen to my King and please listen to me. We are all that stands between The Others. Please trust us."

Little Lucy could feel her heart racing as her anger grew and grew until she reached out with her hands and pulled the garden spider off of its web. How could she trust something so grotesque and so unwelcome. She had to make a statement to Steve, to this so-called 'Spider King'. She knew that he would be watching, so she had to be sure that he got her message and gave up on his plan to live in this house as an equal. Protection was her job, not his.

Little Lucy clasped the body of the garden spider in between her fingers on one hand and then with her other hand she began to pull their legs off. The spider tried to wriggle free and even looked to be trying to bite the hand that was holding it, but thankfully Little Lucy's gardening gloves were too thick for the venomous fangs to get through. She thought she could hear the spider screaming for mercy, promising to leave the garden and never return, but Little Lucy blocked out their cries. This would teach the spider, and no doubt teach Steve too, that their garden was perfectly fine without them. The spider went limp in her hand a bit too quickly though and Little Lucy, disappointed, dropped the spider's body onto the ground and ground it into the grass underneath her feet. Even if the spider did try to come back, it would be too disfigured now to be able to try and take up residence in Daddy's roses again.

Daddy reappeared with some smaller gardening tools just for Little Lucy and the two of them spent the majority of the day tidying up the garden. They made sure that all fallen leaves and petals were swept away from the base of the plants and made sure to scatter plant food and fertiliser throughout the garden to ensure that the plants all grew to be big and beautiful over time. Little Lucy went to bed achy but proud of her work, most notably that she had managed to show Steve and his stupid little family that her family did not need him to help them in any way. The garden was safe because she and Daddy looked after it. They did not need Steve, nor any of his stupid threats or minions.

The next day Little Lucy was awoken by angry cries and a lot of cursing throughout the house. Little Lucy left her bed and looked out of her bedroom window, which looked out over the garden. There she saw Daddy, his hair a mess and his face creased in grief and frustration as he looked around his garden. The rose bush looked wilted and brown and the vegetable patch seemed to be rotting before Little Lucy's eyes. But then Little Lucy was brought back from her thoughts when Mummy let out a cry of shock from the bathroom. Little Lucy investigated and saw that Mummy was looking towards the corner of the bath-tub, where there was a small gap between the bath basin and the edge of the wall. The gap was no more than a sheet of paper, and yet as Little Lucy followed

Mummy's gaze, she saw a tiny silver flash disappearing into the gap.

"I really hate those silverfish bugs." Mummy said with a shudder. "Wait here and I will go and get some lemon spray to spray around the bathroom. Hopefully that will keep them out of here."

Little Lucy watched the area where the little bug had disappeared. She stood silently and after a few moments, a silverfish reappeared from under the bath and was making its way towards the back of the sink. The little bug seemed to swim across the floor, its silver body waving side to side like a fish as it moved speedily across the tiled floor. It drew closer to the sink and Little Lucy backed away. While she was not scared of the bug, there was something in its movements that unsettled her and she did not want to get too close to it. But as she stepped away, a large spider appeared from behind the sink and sprang on the silverfish. It appeared to bite down on it, which seemed to kill the silverfish instantly and then it quickly dragged the body back behind the sink.

Here we go again, Little Lucy thought to herself as she angrily knelt down to try and look behind the sink. She pressed her head as hard as she could against the wall and could just make out the very faint outline of the spider. It did not seem to notice her. Was this the bathroom spider that Steve had told her to expect the other night?

Little Lucy felt beside herself in annoyance. She had told Steve that they didn't want his help and yet he had still sent the spider in the garden. Little Lucy had done what needed to be done and killed that spider, making it very clear to Steve that he and his horrible little army were not welcome here. Yet he still thought it wise to now send this minion into her home once more? Clearly her last message had not been loud enough for Steve to hear, buried away in the attic where he hid like a coward whilst sending out his lesser spiders to try and teach Little Lucy a lesson. Well, now she would get very creative and make it clear once and for all that spiders were not welcome in her home.

Little Lucy reached a hand behind the sink and gripped what felt like dust in her hand. When she removed her hand, she had the spider clasped in her fist. Its legs were insanely long and thin, and whilst she could see the legs flailing against her hand and beating as hard as they could in protest, all she could feel was the very faint tickle against her skin.

"I mean you no harm." The spider now seemed to whisper to her, its voice soft and peaceful. "But if one of these silverfish gets in, it will bring others with it.

Without me as a deterrent, more will come and your house will become infested."

"I have already told your king and your friend in the garden that you are not welcome here." Little Lucy snarled back to the spider. It seemed to wilt under her gaze.

"We don't want to take over." It said finally. "You won't even know that we are here. We work in shadows, in secret, to protect your home and thus protect our home. We only want to live in peace with you and your family. We would not harm you."

"Yet are you not invading the house? You want to keep out these silverfish for fear of larger numbers, but what about you and your kind? I will tell you what I told your garden friend. You are not welcome here. And your King needs to pay attention, unless he wants to lose any more of his people."

Little Lucy stood and dropped the spider out of her other hand and into the porcelain sink below her. Little Lucy watched as the spider wandered around the base of the sink, trying to figure out a way to climb up one of the smooth sides to try and get back to its lair. The spider stopped moving as Little Lucy's shadow fell across the sink, and remained still even as Little Lucy gave the sink faucet a tiny little twist. A few droplets of water began to drop down into the sink. The spider was perched a little way up the basin as that was as far as it could climb on such a smooth surface. The water droplets were not a threat but the spider seemed to know that if the droplets kept coming then they would be in very serious danger.

Little Lucy smiled as she slowly turned the faucet a little further. She moved the faucet so slowly that the droplets were gradually increasing in size and speed. Soon, a very thin trickle of water began to continuously pour into the sink and Little Lucy smiled as the spider realised the danger and began to panic. It tried to claw its way up the sink basin but could still not get a firm grip with any of its eight feet, and each time it slipped, it slipped closer and closer to the steady stream of water that was now pouring down the drain. With a small giggle of amusement, Little Lucy turned the faucet with all of her might and a huge stream of water gushed out into the sink, sending tidal waves up the edge of the basin and sending water droplets splashing high into the air so that even Little Lucy felt the cold slaps on her face. If the spider was calling for help, she did not care to hear it. The water caught the spider on one of its outstretched back legs, and the spider was dragged into the current as the water circled the drain. Little Lucy turned off the faucet finally and watched with great satisfaction as the spider was pulled around the whirlpool of the drain, the legs flailing pitifully as it tried to find anything to hold onto, and was then finally sucked down into the piping.

Little Lucy stood triumphantly over the sink, watching the last few droplets of water trickle down the basin towards the drain. Out of the corner of her eye she saw movement and looking back towards the bath, she saw eight, big black eyes staring at her from a crack on the side of the bath where the silverfish had originally come from. Steve would see this. And now maybe Steve would finally listen to her. But her gaze was interrupted as Mummy reappeared in the bathroom doorway.

"Come on Lucy, we have to head out now. Daddy is in a right mess." Mummy said as she gestured for Little Lucy to leave the bathroom.

"What's wrong with Daddy?" She asked with worry.

"Oh Daddy is fine, but it seems he's got a bit of a problem. Some bugs have eaten through all of his vegetables and his flowers. So the garden is useless now. He'll have to start over from scratch." Mummy said with an exasperated shrug of her shoulders. "We're off on an emergency trip to the garden centre."

Little Lucy followed Mummy out of the bathroom, her gaze instinctively looking back over her shoulder. The eight eyes were now gone.

THE NEXT DAY DADDY SPENT MOST OF THE day frantically trying to fix the garden, but every time he came into the house for a drink he looked tired and defeated. The aphids appeared to be multiplying before his very eyes and trying to relocate them or remove them seemed to be a fruitless effort. Mummy had taken Little Lucy into the attic to do some painting, in an attempt to keep Little Lucy occupied but also to keep her out of Daddy's way whilst he fretted silently in the garden.

"Oh no no no no." Mummy wailed to herself as she frantically searched through her piles of canvases. She had a pile of plain canvases, all waiting to be turned into creative masterpieces, and then had her finished works propped up around the attic like a mini gallery. Mummy flew from pile to pile, pulling out different canvases and painting to inspect them closer and then threw them onto the floor in a panic. "Oh no no no."

"Mummy what is it?" Little Lucy asked, heading over to the pile of paintings that Mummy was piling up at her side. Little Lucy picked up a small photo frame sized painting of a county village, and noticed little holes were dotted around the painting, as though someone had been poking holes into the art work. She felt sadness and anger swell in her as she saw the jagged, ugly holes that now ruined the peaceful scene Mummy had painted.

"I think we have moths in here!" Mummy said with despair. She pulled a row of paintings away from the wall where they had been resting and as she did, two moths emerged from behind them and began to flit around the room in a bit of a daze. "Oh no oh no." Mummy kept whimpering to herself. She danced on her toes slightly as she thought of what to do and then in a mild panic, she ran to the small window and threw it open. She returned back to the stacks of paintings and began waving her hands frantically at the moths, trying to lead them towards the open window and away from any more of her beloved paintings. Little Lucy jumped up and she too began to frantically wave her hands in the air, trying to shoo the flying pests out of the room.

They may have looked ridiculous, but somehow it worked and the moths left through the window. Mummy gave Little Lucy two big high fives and a small cheer before turning back to survey the room, sitting herself down on the floor to sort through what could be saved and what was entirely ruined.

Little Lucy noticed that one of the moths however appeared to be stuck on something at the very top corner of the window. Little Lucy looked up and could see that the moth had gotten a wing stuck to a piece of web. Little Lucy could just make out the web, as it glittered ever so slightly when the sun beams hit it at a certain angle. Little Lucy watched as a thick, black spider started to emerge from wherever it had been hiding in the corner. As the moth flitted and tried to free itself, the spider made its way across the web and pulled the moth closer via the silk string it was attached to. Little Lucy watched as this spider bit the moth and then began to wrap it up in a silk cocoon, no doubt saving it for later.

Was this Steve's last attempt to show Little Lucy that spiders could be helpful? Little Lucy watched the spider, her blood echoing in her ears as she tried to contain her anger. Steve had seen what she had done to the spider in the garden, and had seen what she had done to the spider in the bathroom, so why had he still sent this one to her home? Had she not proven to him that they were not necessary, that they did not need the help of spiders to keep their house clean? Had she not made it very clear to him now that Little Lucy did not want Steve or any of his eight-legged minions in or around her home? What was it going to take to make this point to Steve and to make him just leave Little Lucy and her family alone?

Little Lucy reached up and without thinking about it, she swept the spider into her hand. She opened her hand to look down at the spider, which was small but thick, with a large abdomen and eight thick very dark brown legs. It looked up at her with its eight eyes pleading.

"I am the last defence. The last warning. While they may get in, they will not be able to leave and so cannot bring The Others back with them again. Not whilst I am positioned here outside of the house. Please, let me do my duty. Let me protect this house in the tiny way that I can. Please, let me live." The spider stared at her, its voice soft but strong as it tried to plead its case.

"You know I can't let that happen." Little Lucy responded. Something stirred in her, as though she almost felt pity for the tiny creature in her hand. She thought about how she would have felt had someone tried to remove her from her home or tried to stop her doing what she wanted, and she felt a sharp pang of guilt for the other spiders she had killed in the past three days.

"You can throw me out of the window if you would like." The spider said, as though sensing her hesitation. "If I survive the fall, I can set up somewhere more secret. You won't even know I am there. You will never see me again. Nor any of my species again."

Little Lucy studied the spider for a moment longer, and whilst she felt resistance rise in her, she knew what she had to do. If she didn't, Steve would have won. Because she felt like it was just a game to Steve. How many of his people had he sent to do his dirty work whilst he hid somewhere deep within the house. Little Lucy had made her position clear, that this was not a fight that Steve would win, yet he had not said anything to her directly. He had sent his warriors to try and reason with her and each one had met a gruesome death. But maybe Steve needed a bigger message.

"Your King seems to know what he is doing. See if he will help you now." Little Lucy replied coldly and she placed the spider back on the windowsill. The spider stared at her for a moment, clearly unsure if it was to make a run for it or not. In that moment, Little Lucy was able to place two of her fingertips onto the spider and she began to press down. One fingertip pushed down on the thick abdomen, whilst the other pressed down on the spider's head so it could not lift itself up fully. Its legs flailed underneath the pressure but it could not slip from underneath her fingers. She pushed harder, and could hear the spider calling out for its king, for its people. Calling for help. Calling to her for mercy. Little Lucy watched as the spider flattened further beneath her strength and then, like a balloon, she felt the small body pop underneath her hand. She raised her hand and saw the yellow goo that was pooling around the broken body of the spider, its legs twitching as she swept it over the edge of the windowsill. She had wanted to hear the satisfying thud of the body hitting the ground, but that would not happen. But at least she knew that Steve would be able to find the body. What more of a message could Little Lucy send to him?

"Lucy, what on earth have you got on your hands?" Mummy came over when she saw Little Lucy still stood by the window, admiring the mess on her hand. She looked at the mess and grimaced. "Let's go wash your hands first. We need to clean these window sills at some point too, they're absolutely filthy."

Mummy led Little Lucy downstairs and into the kitchen where Daddy was standing over a pot of boiling water.

"I was going to make us some dinner, if you fancied it?" Daddy said. He was sunburnt and sweaty, and looked very tired after a long day in the garden again.

"Oh yes please!" Mummy said happily as she began to wash Little Lucy's hands. "We also need to buy some more repellent I think. Some moths got into the attic. Most of my paintings will need to be redone."

"What is up with all of the bugs lately?" Daddy muttered with a concerned frown on his face. He reached down into one of the kitchen drawers in front of him and pulled out a box of dried pasta. He opened the half closed lid and then with a shriek of his own he dropped the box onto the floor as he leapt backwards. He said another bad word loudly in surprise and then Mummy repeated it too in disgust.

The box of pasta seemed to be alive and when it hit the floor, the box fell to the side and threw a mixture of pasta and silverfish into the air and across the floor. Mummy pushed Little Lucy back as the silverfish panicked and began darting about in all directions looking for a safe hiding place. Daddy was trying to reach for a broom or a towel or just anything possible to try and sweep the bugs and the fallen pasta back into the box so that he could get rid of them. Little Lucy however was distracted by the small cluster of moths that were now flitting through the kitchen.

That night Little Lucy could not sleep again.

Mummy and Daddy had spent the rest of the day putting repellants around the house and throwing away the majority of the dried food that they had in cupboards as more and more silverfish seemed to have made their home within the depths of the kitchen cupboards. The family had shut all windows and Mummy had spent most of the day adding extra sealant to all doors, windows and cracks around the entire house to try and keep the new pests out. Little Lucy knew what was happening, even if Mummy and Daddy did not.

At least she thought she did, until she was awoken that night by a strange tickling sensation across her whole body. Still half asleep, she twisted and turned in her covers but the tickling would not stop. Then parts of the tickling turned to itching, which eventually got so bad that she had to sit up and see what was bothering her. Her hands felt tingly, her legs felt tingly, and her face and neck were feeling itchy and sore, as though she had a thousand little needles poking at her skin but not quite breaking the surface. She rubbed her eyes in the darkness but could not see anything. She leant over to turn on her bedside lamp and blinked at the sudden golden glow that erupted around the room.

Her walls were covered in spiders. Her bedroom floor was covered in spiders. Her dressing table and her wardrobe were all covered in spiders. When she looked down she saw that even her bed was covered in spiders. She went to push the covers away but even under the covers were more spiders. She looked at her hands and saw the spiders crawling up and down her arms. She could feel them underneath her pyjamas, going up and down her back and across her legs. She could feel them through her hair and across her scalp. She would have screamed had she not been scared that the spiders would crawl into her throat to choke her. She was scared to even blink for fear that there too would be more spiders, hiding behind her eyelids.

There were all sorts of spiders. Big ones, small ones, green ones and black ones. Some were hairy whilst others were decorated with stripes or circles across their abdomens. They were hung from the ceiling by invisible strings of web. Some were carrying balls of webs across their back, and even these balls seemed to squirm with the hundreds of baby spiders that lurked within them. They were all moving closer and closer towards her, as if they were all going to wrap her in their silk and devour her overnight. Little Lucy wanted to scream in horror and disgust but the fear of being choked by spiders made her lips glue shut. Little Lucy was trying to find the power to run from the room when a voice echoed through her head.

"You ignored him." It sounded like a thousand different voices all speaking at once until it was as loud as someone shouting directly into her ear. "You did not listen to the King, and now you must suffer the consequences. We will leave your house for good, and it will be up to you to save your family from The Others."

Little Lucy could stand it no more. This must just be a bad dream and if she could just force herself out of the bed she would be able to flee from this nightmare. She shut her eyes tightly, feeling the sharp tickles of feet running across her eyelids as the spiders moved across her and she willed her legs to obey her. She took a deep breath and with all of her might she flung her legs over the side of the bed and opened her eyes ready to run for the bedroom door.

But the spiders were all gone. She was alone in her bedroom, with the soft glow of her night light next to her. The walls were the same colour they had always been and her carpet was once more just carpet. She gingerly lifted her hands up to her face and saw the same childish fingers as always. It must have been a dream, she tried to reassure herself. A strange dream induced by the stress of this situation. It could not have been real. Little Lucy ran her hands over her body once and paced her room to make sure there were definitely no spiders. Once satisfied that this was all just a dream, she gathered up her duvet around her and stared into the light of her nightlight until morning came.

THE NEXT MORNING, LITTLE LUCY WAS greeted by Mummy and Daddy scratching at their arms and their necks until their skin was bright red and angry looking. Little Lucy sat at the table in her usual spot and as she waited for Mummy to make her breakfast as usual, she spotted a tiny black dot hopping across the table.

"Oh christ, they're everywhere!" Mummy cried and she slammed her hand on the table. The black dot moved like lightning across the table as Mummy continued trying to hit it. But as Little Lucy watched Mummy's desperate movements, more little black dots came into her view. They hopped across the table, along the floor, even along Mummy's outstretched arms. Mummy threw her hands up in despair, shaking them violently as she tried to remove the little black dots from her body, before crying in defeat. "I'm having another shower. Lucy, have your breakfast and then you too can go shower."

"But I had my shower last night." Little Lucy protested.

"I know you did, but we all need extra washing today." Mummy said, her voice tired and strained as she walked past Little Lucy and headed towards the bathroom.

"But I don't shower until bedtime." Little Lucy whined to Daddy, who was still scratching away at his body as he choked down his own breakfast.

"Well now we all have to shower twice a day." Daddy responded meekly. "At least until the house is clean again."

Little Lucy leant back in her chair and watched as more little black dots jumped across the table. She looked around the kitchen and saw that the black dots seemed to be everywhere: On the kitchen counter, in the fruit bowl, on the floor and across the cabinet handles. They moved so quickly that Little Lucy couldn't possibly keep count of them all. For every one that she managed to focus on, it seemed that another ten would appear around it, each one moving so quickly that it was impossible to keep up with. Little Lucy felt the faintest of tickles on her hand and when she looked down there were at least twelve black dots running around on her hand and up her arm. She shrieked and flung her arm to the side, visions of last night's nightmare coming back to haunt her anew.

"Come on, shower time. I am done with all of these fleas." Daddy said, his face wrinkled slightly in disgust as he too noticed even more of the fleas around him.

Little Lucy showered first, Mummy and Daddy standing in the bathroom with her to make sure she washed her hair fully and really gave her skin a good scrub. Little Lucy watched as the soapy water ran down the drain, with thousands of tiny black dots trapped in the water. She heard Mummy and Daddy talking in hushed tones about the chemicals they would likely need to buy and what time they needed to be out of the house for the fumigator to arrive. Little Lucy shook her head as she tried to ignore the flash-backs to her nightmare. It had only been a silly dream. Hadn't it?

The shower did nothing. As soon as she stepped out of the water to dry off, black dots would appear on her skin again. Her skin soon became covered in little black dots that would leave behind tiny red dots that made her skin itch like crazy. It seemed like their house was infested with these dots. The only place that they didn't seem able to reach was the shower, but this was only when the water was running.

Little Lucy followed Mummy and Daddy down-stairs and out of the front door. Mummy and Daddy, and now Little Lucy, were constantly scratching them-selves from the itchy bites that were covering their bodies, and Mummy and Daddy were beginning to snap at one another.

But they barely made it out of the door before Mummy and Daddy were shrieking in horror. Their front garden was in tatters. It was a very small front area, possibly only a few steps to get from the front door to the front gate that led onto the main street. But there had been a small patch of grass on the left that Daddy had used as his own little 'wildling' area. He had littered some seeds onto the grass and had largely left it alone, aside from the odd bit of watering in the very hot summer months. The little garden thrived by itself usually, with all manner of bugs and flowers that seemed to bloom all year round. To the right of the little area, were a few potted plants that Daddy used to grow various flowers that would not fit in the back garden.

But these were all gone. The few remaining flowers that were still in bloom were filled with holes, with a few of the stems littered on the ground as though something had chewed straight through it. The wild flowers were all gone and even the grass seemed to have been reduced to flat stubs in the ground, so short that all Little Lucy could really see was the dirt beneath it. And yet the whole area seemed to be wriggling. The entire garden looked to be covered in a bright orange blanket of aphids that was sweeping its way over every single piece of foliage that it could find. Mummy and Daddy shrieked at the sight, with Daddy picking up Little Lucy and all three of them bolting through the garden gate and onto the pavement.

Yet as they did, Little Lucy felt like her skin was crawling. She looked down to see that all of the fleas that had been on Daddy were now migrating to her, and she could feel the soft thuds against her skin as the fleas from Mummy also hopped across to Little Lucy's skin. There were now so many on her that she felt like a thousand needles were being pressed into her skin, as more than a thousand little mouths bit into her skin and began to feast on her. She began to flail to get the bugs off of her skin, but that was not doing anything to shift the fleas.

Little Lucy twisted and flailed so much that Daddy had to put her back down on the sidewalk. Daddy and Mummy then began to try and sweep the fleas off of her, running their hands as gently as they could across her face to remove the pests from their daughter. But every time they waved a handful of the bugs away, more would take their place and swarm even more viciously. Little Lucy flailed her arms even more aggressively, spinning on the spot to try and disorientate or dislodge them. But with every step she took, she could feel more bugs crawling up her skin. Bigger ones. Hungrier ones.

Little Lucy looked down at the pavement to see giant beetles, long spindly earwigs and sparkling silverfish crawling towards her all along the street. Above her head she saw moths gathering like a dark storm cloud and began to descend upon her like a monsoon. She backed herself closer to the front gate to try and avoid the bugs swarming towards her but that just gave the writhing blanket of aphids an opening to join the feeding frenzy. She reached out a hand to steady herself, her eyes fixed in horror at the hundreds of creepy crawling bugs that were rushing towards her like a wave of torment and as her hand touched the wooden gate she could feel a ripple as the aphids from the garden snaked their way up her arm and across her body. Little Lucy could do nothing but watch as her body was enveloped by every bug that seemed to live in the local area, as her parents watched on in stunned, horrified silence not knowing what was happening or what to do. Little Lucy could feel her body being lifted, but could not see where. The bugs were now all over her face - she could hear an earwig hissing in her ear as though laughing at her. She could feel a silverfish trying to climb up her nostril and a blanket of the aphids were obscuring her vision as they climbed over the eyes and into her eyelashes. She shut her eyes tight and tried to ignore the digging of their feet against the tops of her eyelids. She then felt herself surrounded by an unknown pressure, as though she was being pulled through a very small gap, and then the light disappeared completely and she was left in darkness, with only the mocking pain of her bug cocoon for company.

LITTLE LUCY OPENED HER EYES AND FOUND herself in a dark, damp and musty smelling area. It was small and cramped but there was a smell that felt familiar to Little Lucy in some way. She tried to move her body but it felt heavy and odd to her. She could not feel her fingers or her toes and could only feel the fiery itching from the bites across her body. She tried to sit up, but her body felt too weak. She turned her head to look around herself.

It was dark aside from a small slit in the wall. She craned her neck and could just make out the familiar sightings of the attic. Was she inside the wall? But she couldn't figure it out quick enough as a black cloud seemed to obscure her vision and the slit in the wall was hidden from her. IT was the first time she also became aware that she was not alone. A few inches away from where she lay, there was a ring of bugs around her, all of them hissing and spitting and clawing at the ground to get to her. She looked around and saw that these bugs were covering every last millimetre of the room, from the walls to the ceiling, and some areas were so compacted with bugs that they were crawling over one another trying to get the best view. She very slowly tried to lift herself up onto her elbows to get a look at her legs, and when she did, she saw that the bugs had created a ring around her and seemed to be held back by an invisible barrier.

"Awake at last." A voice, low and slow, was coming from just above her head. Little Lucy looked up to see Steve slowly descending towards her from above, a thin thread of webbing allowing the spider to slowly float down. Little Lucy tried to back away, but there was no space for her to move. She tensed herself as the huge spider gently lowered itself onto her chest and walked casually down her torso before resting on her belly. The spider turned to look at her, eight eyes flashing red in the darkness and two shining white fangs poised at her.

"Get off me." Little Lucy said in fear. "Where am I? What do you want?" Steve was now sitting on her, as though there was nothing wrong with such an unjust and disgusting act. His hairy legs were pressing into Little Lucy's torso as he sat there brazenly. Little Lucy tried to wiggle free, or at least make him move off of her, but Steve just continued to stare at her coolly through eight, unblinking eyes. She had thought Steve was a monstrous size before, but up close he was even more imposing.

"You were warned that this would happen." Steve now said dryly. "I warned you that there would be consequences. I came to you to create peace and you met them with war. Our warriors asked for mercy and yet you responded with torture. You killed them all and there must be justice for that crime." The spider's voice seemed to break slightly at the mention of their fallen warriors. Little Lucy couldn't help but whimper in response.

"But this is my house." Little Lucy said feebly. "We don't want you here."

"This house has, and always will, belong to the creatures that live within it." Steve seemed to spit back. "Generations of creatures have lived within these walls since it was first erected, and before then we lived in the ground that it sits upon. You own nothing."

"What do you want from me?!" Little Lucy now yelled as panic set in. "I'm just a child."

At her words, the walls around her rippled in anger. The bugs did not come closer to her but she could feel their hisses and cries of anger as though they were throwing stones at her from all directions. She looked around at the thousands of bugs that surrounded her and her panic simply increased. She had not envisaged this as her punishment. A few bugs she could have dealt with but this was an army. An angry, hungry army.

"I could just let them eat you." Steve said simply, as though reading her thoughts, as he waved one hairy leg to refer to the magnitude of bugs around the two of them. "I mean they wouldn't eat you, not in one go. No, they would take years to eat you. Take some of your ear whilst you sleep, the skin off of your toes and your fingers. Slowly poison you with their infectious bites that would make you spend the rest of your life scratching away at your skin so hard that you'll eventually rip your own skin off in layers. I could let that happen. I could leave you to the mercy of The Others around us."

"Mummy and Daddy would get rid of them."

Little Lucy said back with as much confidence as she could muster.

"For a short time yes, but they'd be back. They always come back. Some of these creatures have existed before even humans existed and they will continue to exist long after you are all dead." Steve replied. "And no matter where you go from now on, you will be followed. Your mother and father not so much but so long as they stay around you they would still be subjected to the odd bite or scratch now and again. But no matter how many times they move house, or even move country, The Others will follow you and so you will never be rid of them."

"I just wanted a pretty and clean home. A safe home free from spiders." Little Lucy said, tears welling in her eyes.

"We all want a safe home." Steve fixed his eyes upon her now and Little Lucy felt herself wilting before the endless stare. "But you are the biggest threat to this house and to us. Whilst we do not expect humans to love us - even I admit that we can be quite the scary sight at times - we do expect kindness. Yet that is so rare. It is why we hide away. And yet you seemed to go out of your way to cause as much pain and suffering to us as you could. Even though your parents have always been so kind. Your parents always treated us with kindness and respect and yet you always sought out violence. I cannot let you go, because how many more of my family will you murder for sport?"

"None, I promise!" Little Lucy spluttered through her tears. "I promise, I can change."

"I wish I could believe you. But every time you were given the chance to let our warriors go, you still chose violence. You will never change, so I must make you see the error of your ways once and for all."

"What do you mean?" Little Lucy said quietly.

"I will let you live. But with a catch. You wanted to protect this home so badly, so I will leave you to be its *only* protector. We will not help you. We will not support you. And we will all leave as you wished. It will be you, against The Others, for as long as you can hold them back." Before Little Lucy could question this statement further, the house spider reared his front legs up and, with his fangs gleaming, bit down into Little Lucy's abdomen. Pain shot through her body as she began to convulse.

Steve seemed to be growing even bigger. In fact all of the bugs seemed to be growing bigger. Even the room itself seemed to be growing in size. Little Lucy felt the pain coursing through her body and she looked down to see that it was in fact her who was growing smaller. Then her legs split into two, right down the middle, her bones snapping in half as though someone had simply torn a piece of paper. She howled in pain as her arms began to splinter and separate, her bones crunching and snapping as they tore apart and reformed and she twisted in agony as her body writhed and stretched. Her head felt like it might split open too and when she tried to open her eyes against the pain, her vision was blurry and doubled. And then her vision was doubled again and when she could finally focus, she saw eight images before her eyes. She continued to scream as she watched thick, black hair sprout from her torn apart extremities and heard the sickening crunch of bone as new elbows and knees were formed and connected together. She felt her body compress in on itself, as though she was being folded in half and squeezed into a tight ball.

When the pain finally subsided, she was staring up at the face of Steve. She felt even smaller as she stared up at the thick, elongated body of the giant house spider who now towered above her, a look of basic disapproval now clear across his face. At this angle Little Lucy could see the minute details up his face, from the white glow of the two thick fangs that lined his mouth to the separate eight eyes that were all looking down at her with a fiery pride burning deep within them. Steve moved forward, the long legs sending echoes around the small room as his feet thudded with each step as he walked over her towards the wall of bugs.

"Lucy no longer exists. So far as the world is concerned, you never did. Who you are now is who you have always been. You wanted to protect your house. Now you can." He now said coolly. Little Lucy tried to stand but her body felt alien to her. She looked behind her, to see that not only had the spider disappeared into the throng of bugs behind her, but that her own body was now replaced with a dark brown, hairy, round abdomen that had light brown streaks across the middle of it. She tried to stand again but found that her legs and arms now moved as if one, as though she was stuck on all fours. What had happened to her? This had to be another dream, right? This had to be another nightmare that she would soon wake up from, surely. She tried to scream, to call out for Mummy and Daddy, but all that came out was a low whisper of a hiss.

Steve made a clicking sound and the bugs began to disappear, following Steve into the darkness of the room. The small sliver of light appeared before Little Lucy again and she could make out the attic through it. She slowly began to drag herself towards the light.

As she reached out, her arms seemed to be longer with yet more thick brown hair covering them. She couldn't feel her fingers, but she could feel the damp floor of the room against the palm of her hand and that was all she needed for now. So she clawed her way forward, her legs trying hard to push her onwards but still feeling as though they didn't fully listen to her yet.

The slit in the wall did indeed lead Little Lucy into the attic, except it was bigger than she had ever remembered it being. It towered above her, so high that she could barely make out the ceiling. She inched her way further out of the slit in the wall and saw Mummy sitting at her easel, painting away and humming something softly to herself as she did. She looked calm and serene, deep in the moment with whatever she was painting.

"Mummy!" Little Lucy cried out in relief, but the only sound that came out again was a low hiss. It felt unnatural and it burned in her throat. She tried to clear her voice to call out again but this time nothing came out. But she needed to get Mummy's attention. She kept dragging herself closer towards Mummy, and when Mummy finally noticed her out of the corner of her eye she jumped off her stool and yelled for Daddy. Little Lucy thought it was a cry of relief, that Mummy would reach down and take her in her arms and reassure her that this silly nightmare really was just a nightmare. That soon she would wake up safe in her bed and that there was nothing to worry about.

Except Mummy didn't pick her up. She called again for Daddy and then ran as fast as she could down the stairs out of the attic. Little Lucy could only stare after her.

Mummy you have to come back. Little Lucy thought to herself, desperation setting in. Mummy, you have to come back and wake me up. Mummy I can't wake up otherwise. Mummy please, my body hurts so much and I can't chase after you. Mummy. Please. Can't you see that it's me.

And as Mummy disappeared down the stairs, the drumming of a hundred feet echoed from the wall behind her. As Little Lucy turned her head to look behind her, she saw a group of silverfish, huge and hungry and hissing, slowly weaving towards her.

Strangewayes

S. VALENTINE ASTORIA

She is five and her shins are bloody, but the crows are her friends.

They caw to her from overhead, lost in the woods on the way home from the beach, and she follows. The branches in the late afternoon sunlight look like fingers ringed with gold.

She clears the trees and finally sees the familiar sight of her family's ramshackle house beyond the orchard. A raven lands before her in the grass, tilting its head as it searches her with fathomless eyes.

In its beak, it holds a jewelled brooch shaped like a moth, and drops it at her feet. She stows it under her pillow.

When her father finds it, he sells it.

SHE IS SEVEN AND THE APPLES ARE ROTTING on the trees.

With crisp autumn sunlight shining into her red tresses one early October morning, she bites into one as she harvests and a fat, wriggling maggot squirms onto her finger. She watches in fascination as it probes her trembling flesh before finding fresh fruit to sink its mandibles into and squirming back into the core.

She drops the apple only when she hears her mother calling from the house; they have linens to launder. On her way back, she finds a bleached raven's skull nestled in a bed of dry grass and takes it with her.

The wind howling through the orchard sounds like it's calling her name. But her father's voice roars louder when she dawdles.

SHE IS NINE AND THE WINDOWS RATTLE LATE at night.

Every night.

She hears a cracked old voice saying her name, her full name: *Constance Strangewayes*. Opening the window, she finds nothing but rustling in the bushes. It sounds like someone calling her away to the wilds.

When she throws a loose piece of mortar, a black cat skitters into the darkness. She locks the window, but it rattles the next night, and the one after, and every night until the Solstice is passed.

Her father tells her not to answer it.

SHE IS ELEVEN AND THINGS HAVE BEEN QUIET for a while, except for last night.

A fierce storm blew in from the sea. It uprooted half the orchard, waterlogged the ground, slicked the road. Her father slipped and shattered his knee.

Her first blood came that tumultuous night, and when her mother caught her stuffing moss wrapped in linen into her undergarments in the morning, she chastised her for hiding it.

The hot day festers like a greening wound in the humidity that rises from the water, sailing towards a swarming evening, but when the stars come out, she sees her face in the constellations.

Her mother collects the moss into a clay jar. She adds the raven skull. She adds rosemary and wine, pins from her sewing kit and nails from the old barn. She takes it behind the house and buries it, somewhere dark, somewhere secret.

But Constance watches from her window, she sees her mother tuck it under the cornerstone. For protection.

SHE IS THIRTEEN AND SWOLLEN WITH pregnancy. It wasn't her choice.

Her mother refuses to look at her. She can't tell her who, because it wasn't any of the village boys. There's no one to marry to make her decent.

Spawn of the devil, the townsfolk say.

Her father says nothing, leaning on his cane.

Her mother gives her a foul-smelling tincture and the bleeding starts. It's the worst pain she's ever felt in her life. Her mother whisks away the remains before she can even see what grew inside her for three short months.

SHE IS FIFTEEN AND THE WIND IS SILENT.

It doesn't rush through the blossoming orchard in

the high spring, nor jostle the trees in late summer when the pears are ready to fall.

None of the village boys will marry her. She helps her mother make jams and fresh bread in the kitchen, darns socks by the fire, helps her father salt and smoke the fish in the smokehouse.

She is fifteen and wasted. Her younger sister will make a good wife, when she comes of age, and her father counts the dowry.

She takes her place when his hands wander. She makes sure her sister isn't soiled.

SHE IS SEVENTEEN NOW, ON THE CUSP OF eighteen, and it's happened again.

Her mother cries.

This time she refuses the mixtures, she fights when her father tries to hold her down, bites him.

She runs with his blood in her mouth, spits it in her hand and draws shapes in her palm.

She runs to the beach, and the howling wind that rises sounds like it's calling her name again: *Constance Strangewayes.* Her feet turn numb on the cold midnight shingle as she stares at the fat moon swelling like her belly.

It's smiling at her.

Under the house, she digs until her fingers are numb and her knuckles bloody and her eyes blur with tears, until she finds the bottle she helped her mother bury all those years ago. Earth has moulded to the outside of it during the intervening years of sorrow and rain, but she cracks it off with shaking hands.

With a screech, she throws it at the wall of the house. The old bits of bone and needles and ashes scatter into the rose bushes, and finally, *finally* she breathes.

The wind at her back no longer howls for her, it howls with her, and with its might she throws open all the doors and lets it tear through the house, whisking linens and thread and dust into the sky.

With a second heartbeat thrumming inside her, a new song that resonates in her bones alongside the one she's always known, she points the finger. She screams his name, the name he gave her.

His heart stops in his chest. The holy man buries him the next day, unmarked.

SHE IS NINETEEN AND THE VOICES COME TO her every night. They sing her lullabies in the whorl of ravens in the sky and the whistling owls and the rush of water against the shore.

Her sister is married. Her mother is dead. It's been a long, dry summer.

She still makes jam in the kitchen, darns socks by the fire, smokes fish in the smokehouse. Instead of protections, she buries promises under the corner-stone. Seeds, gleaming coins and sea-tumbled glass.

The wind whistles across the fields behind the house, bending the wheat to its whim, where she sits on the low rock wall with her son. The wilds lie beyond, and the dark, dark sea below, illuminated by flashes of lightning in the far distance.

The storm rolls on. She calls it home.

Don't Shoot the Messenger

CALUM DICKINSON

A word of caution!
In a world of devils, deceit and danger.
Learn from the tales of the cloakéd
    ranger.
Through rugged terrain, both mud and
    gravel.
All manners of darkness, they must
    travel.
Fear not, dear reader, you must not
    despair.
For every shadow cast, lightness is there!

T f ever there was a weather that forebodes of what is to come, it was that fog which shrouded the ground. The fog that knitted together the trees into a wall. The denseness that could only tell you it was day, and not dawn, morning or afternoon. My clothes sticking to me as if I had been in a downpour and not just trapped in a cloud. I hear the creak of the branch as the drips form and fall, allowing the tree to spring back to where it once was. The white blanket cushions the sound when something falls. The dark figures of the trees were no different from the man on horseback.

THE MAN ON HORSEBACK!!!

The wood fiddles in my fingers as I try to load my bow. The notch! Get the notch! Raise it up! Steady! I am forgetting something... What could I be forgetting... Oh yes. Breathe!

The man on horseback did not slow during my mild panic, just trotting forward. There was no hail of greeting, nothing to acknowledge me. The string of my bow threatening to slip from my wet fingers and make the music of one note. I repositioned my fingers, very carefully, before I call my challenge.

"Stand where you are, Stranger!" My tongue felt like it was three times the size in my mouth as I called down. My projected voice was meant to come out commanding, as opposed to an overzealous mouse telling a sauntering cat to stop.

Barely a ripple of muscle from man or beast, nor a whisper, as the horse took a final half step before bringing itself in line. I could not tell if it was the shadows that swayed or the trees. The head of the horse bobbing down, making it look like the man grew taller as the rest of the body became visible. He made no movement, nor sound. I could feel the string tremble under the strain, and this was not even pulling it all the way back.

"State your business!" I should have sounded more in control this time. The cat was not prowling forwards anymore.

The fog parting, as if controlled by this stranger, lingering on the moat, the last barrier between us. I would have thought the rider had come forward if the horse wasn't busy eating grass. The slit for his arms to hold the reins appearing to be the only opening of his cloak. A sword, dull at his side, with an unadorned leather sheath. His boots that seemed to have a longer tale to tell than the wearer, as they held in the straps from the saddle. The hood was what held my attention. That and the chin which seemed to define his face.

Although it was the only part of the face that was visible.

"A word with your Elders", The Stranger responded. A hesitation from me. It was not a purr that I was expecting. No purr to my squeak. There was no excessiveness to the request, although it held an air of authority as the sound travelled up. I was half expecting a request of food, a bed or a barter of trade. I could not help as I threat assessed him to note the lack of saddlebags. Only the sword and horse may have been worth a coin. Maybe he was the offer.

Plucking up the courage to tell him that 'we had no need for sellswords', I could not help feel a calming as the sweet smell of pine needles infused into my nostrils. I could not turn him away simply because I wanted to avoid the whip of our Elder's tongue. I could also not go to the Elder saying that an unknown wanderer had requested an audience. The middle ground then. I would judge whether it was worth the time of the Elder.

"And what may that word be?"

The cold, sharp fingernail of the fog ran down my back. There was no bravado, as he told me. There was no flourish in his words. No grand removal of the hood or presenting of his blade. Simply, there was no emotion of any kind. Only the words.

"The Oclathru, this way Cometh!"

When the Cloakéd Ranger arrived at
   the gate.
He was met by fear rather than hate.
A call from the wall, he responded to
   the ask.
A warning of the Oclathru, was his task.

Oclathru, Destroyer of minds.
Breaker of body, how the soul binds.
Eater of children, Corrupter of the
   weak.
One must fear the coming of the Beak.

"STAY TH..THERE!", CUTTING MY STAMMERING request short at The Stranger, as I fought control over the pit of my stomach starting to turn. He remained motionless, much like the other guard that I was trying to kick awake. The guard slow to rise, probably expecting it being an end of a shift, as we normally took it in turns to watch and catch a sneaky nap. After all, nothing ever happens at this time in the morning. Well, until today that is.

I nodded over the wall, and his eyes bulged at the stationary rider. I hushed him. "Just keep watch. I need to go get the Elder". I did not mention the Oclathru. The less that knew about this, the better. Sleep was gone from my replacement so quickly, there was nothing like fear to remove that morning grogginess.

Heading down the steps from the walls, attempting to hurry while holding back, as a watchman running through the street is not something anyone wanted to see in the morning. It was early enough that there were still wild birds on the streets that took off as I approached. Feeling sparks ripple across my skin from the banging of shutters being opened. My nose being affronted by the stale smells that wafted from the dwellings. It reminded me why I often stayed a little later on the wall. Let a breath of air get through the streets first. Although, while it was an offensive smell going up one nostril, the other had that sweet and savoury smell of freshly baked breakfast on the go. Now I could not tell if the movement in my stomach was from fear, repulsion, or hunger.

After stepping in as many puddles as I had dodged, puddles of unknown origin as it did not rain last night, I reached the large double oak doors of the building that once housed the King. Guards no longer blocked your entrance. Now you could come and go as you please. Well, if you had no good reason, it probably would not be the best idea to enter or you would face the wrath of the Elder. After being surrounded by the white mist on the wall and the brown of the mud of the street, the colours of the tapestries inside burned into my eyes in wonder. It did not matter how many times I passed through to the throne room; I was always in awe. Gone were the smells of the outside, now only the metallic scent of burning torches that squeezed the inside of your throat.

Pushing the door open to enter the throne room, the wood cooled my hand. No man would ever knock again to enter after the removal of King Levi. Once told as the bravest of men, who slayed an Oclathru with his spear and took the egg as prize, which now stood on the right of the empty Beaked Throne. A solid and ornate throne, topped with the skull of the Oclathru, that was never to be sat on again. The Elder, who stood on the left-hand side of the throne, in front of the spear of Levi, was indicative of that. It does not matter what brilliant feats you could achieve, if you ruled with too heavy a hand then your reign was short. Even his deeds were now questioned by the Elder. Was the egg just a rock and the skull just happened upon?! No magnificent battle to solidify the rule.

"Fabhain? What brings you here?", a note of irritation held in the air. Free to roam wherever you go, as long as it does not annoy the Elder.

"The Oclathru, it comes!", I exclaimed. I could not hold back the emotion like The Stranger. There may have been some waving of hands as a flourish when I gave in to fear-driven excitement at passing on the news.

The Elder shaking his head, "We have given the harvest blessing, and no Oclathru has even stepped to our walls. What makes you think there has been a change?" There was a bit of derision there, but that was the case all the time with the Elder.

"The stranger at the gates has told so, and they have requested an audience."

The Elder's eyes widening was the reaction I had been hoping for when I told the first bit of news.

*Our belovéd King Levi, on the Beakéd
    throne.
Their rightful place, now ash and bone.
A timely gift to the eggless mate.*

Be thee warned if it comes too late.

WE HAD MARCHED THROUGH THE STREETS IN silence, with myself having to do a few hops and skips to keep up. I may be wrong, but this awkward way of walking and paying less attention to my feet seemed to make me miss more puddles of questionable substance. Whether it was the Elder being out this early, or news starting to spread about a stranger outside the town's gate, people were starting to follow along. What started off as one or two soon became a cacophony of splashes and slops behind. Very few puddles would remain after this, just a well-mixed slurry that used to be a path.

The Elder climbing up the wall with complete abandon; it was worth reminding myself that the Elder was not an old man. We chose him for a reason. Not just for his mind, but his skill with the blade. The guard who I had left in my place was still on alert, but as I looked over the wall, The Stranger had dismounted. His horse eating at the grass at the side, with The Stranger standing in the same place that I left him. The guard, who moved back to allow the Elder could be directly opposite The Stranger, was not given the same courtesy with barely an acknowledgement. The stench of mud drifted up to me as the Elder turned his nose at the sight of the outsider.

"Say your piece and leave," The Elder called down.

Now, my mother always taught me to never turn away someone from sustenance and shelter. Even, and especially, an outsider, so this rankled me. I had to balance that with my fear though. Not so much of The Stranger, but the news that he brought. Looking over to the Elder, simmering while waiting for a response from down below. I realised I was also not speaking out of fear of his wrath too.

The Stranger replied, "You are asking me to deliver the message from over the moat?" and seemed to have no issue in projecting his voice. Many of those that stood behind the wall. It would be the first time hearing an outside voice other than a passing trader.

"I can hear fine where I am!" The Elder challenging back with one of the more stern faces and stances that I had seen from him.

"As you say," as The Stranger removed his hood. Now, when he had first emerged in front of the wall, the mist had evaporated like there was no memory of it. In the same way, so did the mystery and any intimidating persona was gone when the unhooded face looked back. He was young, very young, nearly half my age, and I could not help having a pang of jealousy. He was riding free across the countryside and I was stuck guarding a wall of a town. "The Oclathru heads this way."

I held my breath as I remembered him delivering the warning and my first reaction. I could feel the movement of the crowd behind me suddenly stop. All those little sways, the breathing, the rubbing of clothes. All stopped. Frozen at that moment. Until the laughter came.

There was no fear in The Elder, and his laughter soon caused the crowds to start murmuring. "And why should we believe you, boy?" He turned with his back to The Stranger and addressed the crowd of townsfolk. "Do not worry, it is the raving fantasies of a child," which brought about snorts and smirks.

The Stranger showed no sign of annoyance at being ridiculed. No arrogance before calling back up. "That would be your folly. I only deliver the warning. Do with it as you wish." With a click of the tongue, his horse raising its head from foraging and sauntering over while still chewing away. The wet moss dug in under my fingernails as my body reacted to the tension by gripping the wall.

I saw the Elder's face go red, as The Stranger taking hold of his horse's reins and starting to turn away was seen as a slight. It was for the Elder to say when they were done, he may have wanted to mock more. "You threaten me!" perceiving it as a threat came as a bit of a surprise to me. I could only see it as a warning of something that was going to happen. That did not seem to matter with the Elder, who took it as a personal threat and not even towards the town.

Now, maybe it was the fact that The Stranger took no heed of the anger. Or it was the hood going back over, transforming him into someone to reckon with. Whatever it was, the Elder's anger increased, storming off the wall, down the steps and I could hear him demanding the gate to be opened.

The Cloakéd Ranger at the gate stood
    tall.
A warning of danger he did call.
The mocking, the anger and the frown.
The actions of one man had doomed
    this town.

Tempers flare with madness soon.
On the night of Oclathru's moon.
Eyes wild and full of craze.

Marks the beginning of end of days.

THE MOMENT THE ELDER WENT ON HIS tirade, the sun broke through the clouds. Not all areas were lit equally, causing almost a halo effect on the ground where The Stranger stood. The dew on the flowers glistening causing temptation for his horse, the promise of eating again. I could not help admire the discipline in the control he had over his horse. My hands still gripping the wall, not sure whether I should follow the Elder or stay where I was.

The grating of metal on stone of the gate being pulled up rippling through me. The Elder's shouts of impatience at the guard while still going on about the dishonour that The Stranger was showing him. I could not see any of this as it was occurring under my feet, instead just waiting for him to emerge down the path. The Stranger whispered to his horse, as the sun spread further, lighting up the surrounding trees. He took a step in front of his horse as I saw the Elder approach.

Spots momentarily covered my vision with a flash of light. A blade. The Elder's blade. As he drew it, catching the sun, hitting the beam straight back at me. Crossing the distance at speed, ranting unintelligibly.

The Stranger dropped his horse's reins and took a further step forward. Hood still drawn and no indication of going for his sword. My chest tightening, body reacting to the tension, with my throat tightening in preparation for being sick.

With an arrow being so streamlined, the whisper of flight is so difficult to hear, it is like a silent killer. The whoosh of the sword blade going through the air was more terrifying to me. Both stood still after the swing, the spray of blood between them as the sword finished its arc. He stumbled, although his hood barely moved. No gasp given as he finally staggered back from the Elder, turning to the moat and stepping out as if there was a shining, rippling path. There was no flailing of arms as he fell. His brain had not quite caught up with what happened to him. There was an element of calm in the moment, just before the sound erupted as the body hit the water.

The moat was not the prettiest things of our little town. It is not a water supply we would use; The sole purpose of the moat was to deter those that wish to do us harm. The fetid smell that came from The Stranger breaking the surface was a reminder of this. My skin prickled from the imagined water droplets spraying me, leaving me feel unclean.

"You dare threaten me!", a red faced Elder challenged the floating figure. Spittle went through the air as he foamed with anger. Blood dripping from his blade, pointing at the mark it had made. I could taste the metallic tang of the blood on my tongue as it dripped from the blade.

Turning to the gates, The Elder was looking like he was preparing to address us. The way the Elder could look at the crowd and yet make it feel that you were being the sole focus of his message. His eyes boring a hole into my soul. "Let this be a warning to all those that grace our town." Raising out his hands as the sun went behind a cloud. "We are not to be trifled with. No threatening of us with mythical beasts. Exploiting us. Extorting us. The last man who tried to do that was King Levi. And look how well that turned out for him."

There were some cheers and laughter at this. I found that I could do neither nor say anything. A man was dead for simply bringing news. Each new moon, we paid homage to this beast, even though no one alive had seen one. The only evidence sat in the throne room. The egg appearing in my mind, bathed in light, like The Stranger was right before his death. Now it was a red mist, like the veil that went over the eyes of the Elder, that surrounded The Stranger as he floated face down. I knew well the wrath of the Elder, but I never expected it to lead to a death.

The Sun broke through the clouds once more, shining again on the water. The body in the moat, stirring.

A single strike from a sharpened blade.
A body dropped, that which was slayed.
To any other man, a fatal blow.
To the Cloakéd Ranger, this telling will
grow.

THE ELDER RIPPED THE HALBERD FROM THE guard's grasp, who gave a grunt of surprise, caused my own intake of breath. Swishing in my ears and the halberd twisting in the air, as the Elder expertly spun the weapon until pointing it at the emerging body. The hood hung lower over the face with the extra weight of the water, as The Stranger coughed. The darkened red water moved out like a swirling dancer's dress. Now standing, the water was up to the middle of his chest. A slight movement to the edge was halted with the Elder thrusting the point of the halberd into The Stranger.

He immediately went under. The Elder took a step forward, increasing the pressure. My ears filling with the torrents of a raging river. My eyes were caught in the waves crashing the rocks. My stomach lurched as flailing limbs came out of the swirling, sloshing water in a weird, mesmerising tentacled worship around a central pole. The head managed to pop up a few times, the hood now off as The Stranger pulled up for that life giving gasp of air.

The gasp of life in front of me. The gasp of horror beside me. Or maybe it was my only shock at this. Each time The Stranger managed to breathe, the Elder just pushed harder, moving forward. The strength of the Elder, and the putrid smells from the splashing moat, were equal parts repulsive and impressive. Not many could hold a grown man under water, especially one fighting for their life. To stop moving was to accept death, and The Stranger wanted to live. The Elder, being able to do this at the full length of the halberd too, was humbling.

The dance of the limbs dissipated the blood in the water, making it look like the bleeding was done. The head could no longer reach the surface and the limbs seem to be getting more sluggish. I could think the arms were fish rather than the struggling young outsider. The fish no longer jumping for the insects flying across the water, instead barely breaking the surface as they ate the insects skimming across. Soon, they were swimming just under, with only small currents getting seen. Then they were gone, overwhelmed by the fresh ripples as the stick moved back and forward.

The water calmed and from my vantage point from the wall, I could see the underwater moon of the boyish face behind the green watery sky. Bubbles rising, before getting lost as the Elder thrust a few more times. Fresh blood came into the water and the submerged pale face was lunar eclipsed as the red hue cast across.

Removing the halberd from the water, and instead of going back to the guard, the Elder cast it to the ground, glistening in the grass. The Elder breathing heavily from exhaustion. It must have taken a lot out of him to force The Stranger to remain under water. He went back to the gate, disregarding the horse that had stepped back at the commotion but was now peacefully grazing. The body looked like it would be staying down.

Stuck under water, mud surroundéd.
No longer floating, all agroundéd.
Nobody did anything, no one was brave.
The Cloakéd Ranger ended in a watery
grave.

"I HAVE SAVED THIS TOWN ONCE MORE!", THE Elder addressed the crowd from the wall. It was the easiest area to address the congregated townspeople in the courtyard. "You made a choice for me to lead this town, and I have done so. Not as a tyrant like King Levi and not as a threat like this outsider!" He gestured behind himself. "These men shall never rule again, and unlike them, at your word, I will step aside for the next Elder."

I wondered, always quietly though, as loud wonderings could be dangerous, whether the Elder would step down. Would anyone be acceptable to the Elder as a replacement, and would someone take that risk at potentially becoming a target? All the Townspeople knew his temper, but he had proven there was a reason that he was the Elder to follow. Did I consider it a mistake to kill The Stranger? Of course. The ravings of the Elder as he flew into the rage, I bizarrely found more worrying than the threat of the Oclathru. I could not deny that if The Stranger had been a direct threat, the Elder was well placed to defend.

As the Elder carried on, getting the crowd more excited at his victory, the sun came out from the clouds, warming my face but causing me to close my eyes. I could hear the guards down below making some noise and causing me to turn to see what the commotion was about. As each person out the front followed someone's gesture at the source of interest, they too felt the need to also point to aid the next person. In the moat, The Stranger was afloat and moving towards the bank. With clawing hands, The Stranger pulled himself up the sheer wall of the moat.

It was an impressive feat, with the moat edges having no handholds, and covered with that slimy algae. After all, we wanted people to stay stuck in the moat, designed as a one-way journey. And still he managed to climb, pulling himself onto the solid ground. There was no panting. Nothing to show any use of exertion. Instead, he just turned and looked back at the town he had come to warn. Water pouring off him, as the sodden clothes reached for the ground. There was no anger there, no sadness, not even a look of disappointment. It felt that The Stranger looked directly at me, and with eye contact made, I was sure there was a nod there. A nod of knowledge, of what I did not know.

The hood came up, and The Stranger made the clicking noise, making the horse approach. The Stranger mounted, giving one last look at the town, before turning away. I would have ridden away as fast as possible, but for him, it was a gentle walk, like the one he did when he first arrived. Mist swirled at the feet of the horse again. I felt hands on me, shaking.

"What are you waiting for?!?!" The Elder, his face red, screamed at me, "Shoot him!"

I did not know how long I had been standing there on the wall, not hearing the order from the Elder. The shaking had released me from the trance, as my full attention had been on The Stranger rising from the water and riding away. Wrenching my bow from my shoulder, the Elder thrust it at me, which I instinctively grabbed.

"If he gets away, then he will bring the Oclathru or whoever he serves down on us. He is a demon" loud enough so that the crowds could hear. The Elder was denying the existence one minute of the Oclathru and the next, he was using the thought of it to bring fear and a call to action. The sharp pain in my ribs came out of nowhere. I saw the dagger pressing into me. "Shoot him!" The rest of that sentence, the end

131

of the threat, was all in the eyes as I looked at the Elder.

I knew it was a mistake as I notched the arrow. I knew that The Stranger was not threatening but warning us as I licked the feather, tasting the dry smooth texture. I knew that The Stranger did not deserve this as my fingers pulled back the drawstring. I knew that my life was more important to me as the bow creaked under the tension. I knew that the Elder would kill me as I caught the slight honey scent of ash wood when the arrow went under my nose. I knew that this moment, more than any other time in my life, I would regret. But at least I would live to regret it.

I released the arrow.

The Thud!

The twitching of the ears of the hesitating horse. The rider slumped over and the horse carried on forward, the limp arms no longer holding the reins. I may no longer have the dagger pressed to my ribs, but for what I did, the stabbing pain remained.

The Cloakéd Ranger rose again.
From the water, where he was slain.

A warning he gave, with his ability to
track.
Earned him no thanks, only an arrow to
his back.

I WAS RIPPED FROM MY SLUMBER AS THE BEAK of the Oclathru did the same to my chest. It was the third night of the same nightmare. My mind started to separate dream from reality. The claw around my leg was the twisted blanket. The blood running down my chest was now sweat. I had shot The Stranger in the back, who melted into his horse, before morphing into the Oclathru, launching at me and sending me into the waking world screaming. There was a knock at the door, and I found myself frozen, still terrified that this was part of the dream. At the next knock, I could escape into reality and release my breath. I called for identification and I was told the Elder required my presence.

The Courtyard had an eeriness about it, and I was not sure if it was simply because I was still on edge. My clothes clung to me, fresh sweat still running down my spine. I could not help but think of the salty taste when I washed my face before heading out. I was not being escorted. I could turn and head the other way. Wait until it was light, then go to see the Elder. Through the silence, I could hear buildings settling from the cool of the night. I tried to convince myself it was not an Oclathru watching and clicking their beak. I used all my strength to keep moving forward.

The Elder's eyes were bloodshot, his face red and his chest raised up. Based on the size of the inhalation of breath, I was in for quite a telling off. "You kept me waiting at a time like this?" he screamed at me, pacing back and forward in front of the throne. Black smoke rising from disturbed torches as he walked past them. "I call for you, you come! Do you hear me?"

I was stuck where I had come in. Standing in front of our leader, who does typically get angry when he felt he was not being listened to, but this seemed more than normal. I stayed quiet, and it seemed to be the best option, as I noticed the flushing dropping from his face.

Dropping his head, eyes cast down to the floor. "Clouds of dust on the horizon have been sighted. The Oclathru... It still comes!"

It was like a thing from my nightmare. As the Elder had cast his head down, he was no longer blocking the top of the Beaked throne. The Oclathru's beak appeared to rise from behind, looming over the Elder. I fought my panic of wanting to yell out a warning. It is not real! I tried to convince myself at the same time as shuddering.

"We must prepare our defences. Something to protect us against the Oclathru." This time, it looked like the Elder wanted a response.

I don't know why he brought me specifically. I could shoot an arrow straight, but I was certainly no warrior like the Elder or Levi. The egg was still in a place of prominence. A reminder of the King's most accomplished feat. Paired with the spear on the other side that delivered King Levi from the Oclathru. I doubt I could do that. I don't think I would even have the nerve that Levi had, standing his ground as the monster had charged towards him and pulling the spear up at the last minute. Not many men could, even though breaking would mean death. The Oclathru was said to have poor vision for static objects, picking up movement and by scent. If others stood with me, I may find the courage. My mind drifted to the charging Oclathru. No longer was I standing alone as Levi had done, but now I was part of a sea of spears, standing shoulder to shoulder.

"A wall of spears" I exclaimed excitedly, before more calmly explaining my idea to the Elder. The nod of approval of my plan was encouraging.

"Make it happen," he told me as I already started to think about how much trees had to be felled to make all the spears. Every person in town would need to get involved. The flame beside him flickered again, sending up black smoke once again. I pulled back at the acrid assault on my nose.

"We can also set the black smoke to repel the Oclathru. " I pointed at the torch. The Elder nodded again. I was starting to feel like I could actually be useful.

"If we survive this, then history will sing of us for longer than Levi." There was a gleam to his eye as he looked towards the beaked throne. "You will stand with me and protect me with the bow if all else fails. "

And just like that, my visions of success started to evaporate as I started to imagine the many ways it could fail. The bile of fear filled my mouth.

Three nights pass, and the Oclathru still
  cometh.
How to defend against this behemoth.
The call went through to raise spikes and
  fire.
Else, the town's fate would be dire.

"Fabhain!" they shouted, signalling me to turn, and in one fluid motion, notching the arrow, pulling back the bowstring and let loose at the Oclathru's leg. One arrow to slow, I told myself.

THUNK!

I was already notching the second arrow, not pausing to see if I had been successful, as I took a few steps forward, aiming at the eye. Second arrow was away and flying straight at the target. One arrow to kill.

THUNK!

I gave a snort of satisfaction as my imagined Oclathru went down. The tree stump that was acting as my practice Oclathru was starting to split with my accuracy. There was no shortage of tree trunks to practise on. We had decimated the forest, preparing our defences. Nothing went to waste, though.

I could not help feeling a sense of pride, even with the threat of the Oclathru. Over the days that saw the Oclathru coming closer and closer, we had dented so many axes with the amount of felling of trees for the spears. We had dulled the planes as the trunks became spikes. Many a branch became replacements of the handles broken from the stress of digging the trench. We ate well from the overworked oxen that died from exhaustion at erecting the spikes. The angle of death now pointing towards the growing plume of dust from the Monster's approach.

I could feel the tension, my stomach twisting as I knew that the true test of the spikes would be at the last minute when the Oclathru entered into this valley of trees. The rock-faces at the edge of the forest would force the Oclathru through this pathway. It had no option but to try to jump across the trench. It would have no reason to think it is in danger and spot the char-blackened spikes. The very weight of the beast leading to its own demise. Levi had used the same approach with his lone, flimsy spear. I felt confidence that this would hold up, and even if it did not, we had the pyres ready to go.

Any of the wood that was not used for the spear wall and the tools went to the pyres, split and rapidly dried. We doused shavings in the pitch to give off the noxious fumes. Like the mist, the black smoke would hang in the forest, or rather the stumps of the forest after so much tree removal. The Oclathru, with such a sensitive sense of smell, could never make it through the black cloud and have no option but to retreat. It would not kill it though, but at least it would give us more time to prepare another defence.

And of course, the final last resort was my arrows.

"Fabhain" my name was called once more. I sent another two arrows to my Oclathru, hitting my marks. The wood so badly split, the arrow for the eye went through to the feathers. An earth trembling roar pulled me from my minor victory, and combined with the sound of terror. The Oclathru was in sight.

I had seen the beak on the Beaked throne before, and that is why I am not sure of the surprise at the sheer size of the beast. Maybe it was the rippling muscle, the glint of the talons almost as long as the beak. Maybe it was the short bristled hair that stood on end. The outstretched neck as the beak opened, roaring as it thundered towards us. Whatever it was, I could feel my intestines turning. Others around me were anxiously getting ready to flee, with a small glimmer of hope that our defences would stay strong. Unfortunately, I was so intent on looking at the approach of the Oclathru; I failed to hear the horse's gallop.

The first thing I knew about it was the gust of wind as the horse flew past me. The sweet fragrance of hay and horse sweat as it thundered by. Suddenly, everything else woke up inside me, hearing the horse's hooves clumping. The dizziness as something fast passing so close. The sword gleamed in the midday sun as the rider rode toward the Oclathru. Who was this man who would take on this mighty beast for us? As the rider approached the back end of the spikes, the rider suddenly turned and rode parallel to the spiked defences.

The Snap! The Creak! The Crash! It did not really register with me as the wails of despair took around me. The sword, the rider was slicing through the ropes and the sheer weight of the trunk toppled over, and bridged the trench. The horse galloped away, and although I could not see his eyes, there was no mistaking that it was The Stranger, once again risen from death.

"Retreat!" was the call given. I do not know who it was that made the call, but everyone turned and ran, including me. This was no ordered falling back. It was a panic run to light the pyres before the Oclathru arrived, as it now had a clear path.

Protection raised, with the wall of spikes.
All until the Cloakéd Ranger strikes.
And just like that, hope comes tumbling
down.
Things do not look good, for this ill-
fated town.

WITH BEING AN ARCHER, I WAS OFTEN IN control of my body. Slowing down my breathing, causing everything to relax. It made my movements more fluid and my aiming more intuitive. A monster had never chased me down before this day, and I was finding it quite difficult to get the heart under control. The drums of my chest were playing a rapid tempo as my fellow townsfolk seemingly ran to this beat. Everyone was getting clear before I gave the order to light the pyres. We had left the failed spike wall halfway up the valley path. Now we were at the neck of the bottle as it opened up to the stumps of the decimated forest before our town.

Almost three men tall, the stacks of wood looked no different to the festival fires we used to mark the end of the summer months or celebrate the coming of spring. We would dance around these, where much was drunk and eaten. It was only the two times in the year that all townsfolk knew that they would have enough to eat. This was no celebration, though. These were pyres built out of necessity. Underneath, the black mass of sawdust soaked with pitch. Even unlit, there was enough stench in the air that it gave me the sickly feeling and my mouth was getting that oily film on my tongue in preparation of protecting itself from stomach bile.

I raised my arm as I saw the Oclathru approach and brought it down. At my sign, the assigned men with torches brought them into the pyres. Each of the five pyres caught, and soon the flames were licking the air. The wind whipped through the trees, making tornados of smoke and flame. The black smoke already driving nails into my nose causing me to recoil, moving to a safe distance with the others. As the heat caused the air to shake, the wavy Oclathru paused their advance, further back than I expected. I had thought the Oclathru would have come closer, but the sense of smell was seemingly more sensitive than I imagined. A cheer went up, and I could not help but to join in.

This promptly stopped as behind the pyres, appearing between the flames and the Oclathru, was someone on a horse. My gut lurched as I knew it was The Stranger. The bringer of dread, as my hope evaporated as he rode forward, leaving the pacing Oclathru behind, snapping at the smells. In his hand, he held an apple or a rock. I could not work out why he rode towards us with this. It was difficult to make out through the haze and smoke. As he got closer, I realised it was not solid but transparent, like the outer walls' storm lanterns. Something moved inside, swirling around as flickers of orange and red danced inside it. The Stranger tossed this into one pyre as he rode past.

I often found it strange for them to be referred to as the storm lantern, as although they had shelter from wind and rain, it did not protect them from a powerful storm. If the wind ripped along the wall, we could hunker down to protect ourselves from being cast away. The lantern could not do this, and instead, the wind would pick it up and send the lantern spinning down to the ground below. It was how I was familiar with the popping and tinkling noise of broken glass of whatever The Stranger had thrown into the pyre.

PHOOMPH!

The flames and black smoke went instantly, leaving only a white smoke. It was like the mist that had surrounded The Stranger when I had first seen him, only this time, he was making it. I saw him cast another globe into a pyre.

PHOOMPH!

Same effect. We needed to stop him before it was too late. With two Pyres gone, soon there would be nothing stopping the Oclathru from coming. "Stop him!" I called out as I unslung my bow. No acknowledgement of order. I turned around to find myself alone, as the others that lit the fires were running to the gates. I went to call them back, saying we could still

143

stop him. That three fires would be enough to avoid the Oclathru. My voice caught though, and that moment of hesitation was enough that they seemed too far away for me to call back. I felt my brain dip in the same way it does before slumber takes you.

PHOOMPH!

With only two fires remaining, I joined the retreat. I needed all the time I could get to reach the gate. The Oclathru could soon follow.

Flames a dancing, and rising black
　　smokes.
Burn the pyres so the monster chokes.
The Cloakéd Ranger held aloft a sphere.
Drowned the fires and left only fear.

EVERYONE HAD MADE IT BACK WITHIN THE gates as the Oclathru now made the final approach. It had walked across the trench with the fallen spikes. The smouldering remains of the failed fires no longer repelled it, easily passing the pyres, now devoid of black smoke. The Oclathru came unchallenged. It did not seem to care that we had given offerings to it since the time of Levi. It was coming to our town, and I was now the last line of defence.

I searched for T Stranger, thinking he would jump out at the last minute, but I could not see him. I notched the arrow as I watched the monster coming closer.

"Two arrows," I whispered to myself. I felt the presence of the remaining arrow in the quiver. There were more there, but in my mind it was only one.

I took a slow, deep breath. In and then out to calm me. Do not get distracted by the smell of pine.

I felt the breeze on me, nothing of consequence. Nothing to make me aim differently.

In a state of calmness, I practiced my aim. "One to slow!" as I pointed at the leg and rose slightly, aiming at the eye "and one to kill". The mighty death roar of the Oclathru filled the ears in my mind as the second arrow hit the mark.

I relaxed the string and breathed once more.

"What are you waiting for?" The Elder shouted at me from the courtyard. I tried to drown out all the noise I could, but the Elder's voice made it through. Ignore him! All that matters is the arrow and the target.

The Oclathru thundered towards my line. I

marked my line that I imagined on the ground. Close enough to make the chances of hitting the mark and yet still far enough away that the Oclathru would not be intimidating to both myself and the others in town. I did not want to be jostled around as panic swept through the town. As soon as the first talon passed that line, I pulled back the arrow. Took a calming breath and let it fly.

THUNK!

I already had the second arrow notched as if I had hit the trunk of the practice tree. I rose slightly to the eye and caught my breath when the eye was not there. The Oclathru had risen up on its haunches as I had hit the joint of the front leg and it bellowed in pain.

I calmed!

I reaimed!

I released!

That second arrow flew straight and true, going directly for the eye. I was still holding the firing position as I felt my heart lift. I never noticed the third arrow. Not from my quiver but from the bow of The Stranger. The third arrow also headed to the same mark. To truly appreciate how fast this was happening, we often say things happened in a blink of an eye. Well, let me tell you, I was staring at the Oclathru's eye at that moment, and it barely managed a half blink.

Before this point, I had thought I was the best archer in the world. My arrow being deflected by The Stranger's arrow at the last possible moment suggested otherwise.

"Shoot it again!" I heard from the Elder through my fuzzy blown mind. I barely had the arrow out of the quiver when the whizz of another arrow passed in front of me. I dropped the arrow as my hand slapped to my face, whipped by my broken bowstring, and my bow sprung out of the other. The arrow had sliced my string, snapping the tension of the bow, ejecting it from my grip.

> An arrow shot through the Oclathru's
>   leg.
> The only crime going after its egg.
> An arrow flew true for the eye.
> Once deflected, the end was nigh.

MY FOOTING ALMOST WENT, WALL shuddering as the Oclathru started to climb. With only three legs at full strength, and the wall crumbling under the weight, the Oclathru's ascent was slow. That was what was more terrifying, the steady progress rather than scurrying up. I could not move, stuck to the same spot, not able to leave witnessing the warned horror finally arriving. The squelches of fleeing townsfolk, some yelling, some screaming, and some in a dazed silence. The townsfolk stumbling over each other were counterbalanced by the ones that were supporting the weak.

I could only watch as the Elder cast his eyes around, appearing to shout orders at others. Nobody paying any attention to him. Our eyes met and I think he was shouting something at me, too. I could not comprehend, as all I could feel was the wall underneath me shaking. All I could hear was the talons scraping on stone. The hiss and growl of our impending doom. The Elder started to turn to run, when an arrow suddenly appeared in his leg. The Stranger striding past the whimpering Elder and disappearing into the throne room.

I do not know what it was about The Stranger, but it jolted me out of my fugue state. Even the daylight seemed brighter. The muskiness of the Oclathru in my nose caused me to turn, just as the beak came above the wall. I narrowly avoided a swipe from a taloned leg by jumping back. My foot hitting the edge of the wall and I fell towards the courtyard.

SNAP!

I must have landed on my bow, although it would not matter now since the loss of the bowstring. The pain erupting through my arm temporarily blinding me suggested it was a bone, not my bow that snapped. "Fabhain! Help me!" the Elder called out to me. Through my tears of pain, I got up. Only my left arm appearing to be damaged. I lost my footing once more with the quake from the landing of the Oclathru to the Courtyard. I was powerless as the Oclathru approached the Elder, screaming my name. "Fabhai...."

The beak of the Oclathru stopped the Elder short. An entire head short. The beak turned towards me, dripping with the Elder's remains. Tongue flicking out at me. I pulled an arrow from my quiver, raising it in front, as if it was a sword as I lay on the ground. The feather of the trembling shaft tickled my wrist, and it was with that simple touch my mist of fear evaporated. A feeling of calm swept through me as the Oclathru approached. Before, I was fearful of facing it with only holding a spear. Now, I had a tiny stick to fend off the Oclathru. I could not help but smile as I accepted my fate.

"Hold!" came the voice from behind. The

Oclathru may not have understood the command, more likely turning to the source of the noise. Hood removed, The Stranger held the egg towards the Oclathru. The Oclathru's eyes widened at the sight. Calmly, The Stranger put the egg on the ground, stepping back. The Oclathru keeping a wary eye on us both while scooping up the egg with the injured leg, and using the other three turned and head away. No aggression anymore, and I found myself getting up and just staring.

The Stranger clicked and his horse trotted over. He mounted and started to leave.

"Wait," I caused him to pause. "Why take down our defences but save the town?"

The Stranger did not look back. He just put on his hood and rode away.

The Elder falls with an arrow in leg.
The Cloakéd Ranger gives back the egg.
He mounted his horse and rode away,
Which gives you the lesson for the day.
When messengers come with any news,
Do not shoot, drown or abuse.

The Exiled

EMILY SIGGERS

It was a crisp winter's morning when Ava found the letters. Wylas had left his notes crumpled up at the bottom of his childhood satchel, some parts nearly torn and cutting through his words. She had almost thrown them out; Wylas was always one to scrawl observations about the things he found on their adventures. He was learning, but his idea of trying to help Ava was by making note of each component she'd found, even if the uses he wrote down weren't exact. Dandelions, used as a salve to help those with bloody and sore paws: he wrote about yellow stickers that we rub on fur to help when a claw gets stuck. Wild violet leaves, used to tame hives: were purple buds that we use to stop the red spots.

She always wanted to read these notes when she

had the chance; when Wylas gave her the opportunity to at least. It was always amusing to see where his mind and healing experience were developing and growing. The age of the notes and letters were mostly obvious, the more accurate notes falling into his later teen years.

The first of the notes that she found were evidently from an earlier age, where he was just learning to pick up a charcoal stick between his small paws, the marks smudged onto the page. There were some later notes here as well, some of them that Ava found difficult to read even now, reminding her of...

Choking back tears at the memory, she returned her attention back to Wylas' old bag. She found a crumpled flyer in one of the inside pockets, reading the all too familiar words;

> *By order of the Guild elders, any being seen assisting the Exiled will be subject to trial. Do not help the Exiled.*

She added it to the pile of paper that she had put aside to use as firestarters for the night - there was plenty more where that came from.

Ava had almost finished emptying the bag when she came across a pocket that had been sewn closed towards the bottom. It had been sealed with matching twine to the rest of the bag, so she hadn't noticed it at first, but now she had, it was impossible to ignore.

She took a sharp knife from her own pack and used it to cut one of the sides and pull apart the closed fold. The twine could still be useful, so she pocketed it, amused at the memory of when she chastised Wylas for using the last of it.

The contents of the makeshift pocket were basic - a small horse chestnut conker that made her laugh: years before, Wylas had insisted that it had been taken away by some type of insect, after one went missing during the preparation of a remedy for Mrs Olive. Separate to that, there was a bundle of three pages, the more primitive writing showing that these had been written years ago, when Wylas was smaller. These were different though, they seemed to be more like letters than unique notes, as if he was writing to someone Ava did not know.

She picked up the letters, allowing the satchel to drop noisily to her feet, the conker softly thudding as it fell out on the way down. To her side, the kettle began to whistle from the stove. Quickly she took it off, pouring the hot liquid onto the dandelion leaves that she had painstakingly picked out from the stock that she had once collected with Wylas.

Adding the last ingredients to the remedy, she

settled down next to the cauldron, ready for a few hours of occasionally stirring the mixture. Hopefully this time she wasn't interrupted by every bird or badger asking her for a salve or a potion to cure the most basic of ills. Ava would always help, but the basic remedies reminded her of small Wylas running around, asking her a million questions about what every reagent part did.

Her mind drifted back to the letters - she wasn't doing anything else at the moment, so what was the harm? She unfurled the first one and settled in for the journey of old memories.

THREE DAYS UNTIL WINTER.

IF YOU'RE READING THIS LETTER, I AM DEAD.

FOOLED YOU! I'M NOT SURE THAT THIS IS A DANGEROUS ENOUGH JOB FOR THAT, AVIE HAS BEEN DOING THIS FOR YEARS AND SHE'S FINE. MAYBE THESE 'EXILED' THAT THOSE FLYERS KEEP MENTIONING ARE DANGEROUS – I TRIED TO ASK HER ONCE AND SHE CHANGED THE SUBJECT.

THE GUILD FLYERS DON'T SAY ANYTHING

ABOUT WHY WE NEED TO AVOID THEM, BUT I'M SURE I'D KNOW ONE WHEN I SAW THEM.

I'M WRITING THIS JOURNAL ENTRY IN THE MORNING INSTEAD TODAY, AS IT IS GOING TO BE TOO DARK WHEN WE CAMP FOR THE NIGHT TONIGHT. AVIE IS OUT AT THE MOMENT: SHE HAD TO COLLECT SOME STICKS TO BIND SOME WOUNDS FROM A FEW WEASELS THAT CAME IN LATE LAST NIGHT. THE GIRL HAD BROKEN HER LEG AND IT WAS BLEEDING, SO AVIE PUT SOME WHITE FLOWERS ON IT TO STOP THE BLEEDING, AND THE COUPLE SLEPT ON MY SOFT PATCH FOR THE NIGHT.

I WANTED TO GO WITH AVIE, BUT SHE WOULDN'T LET ME. SHE SAID I HAD TO MAKE SOME KIND OF TEA FOR THEM WHEN THEY WOKE UP. THEY'RE STILL ASLEEP THOUGH, WHICH IS GOOD AS I CAN'T REMEMBER IF SHE SAID NETTLES OR BURDOCK FOR MAKING IT. I'LL HAVE TO LOOK OVER MY NOTE COLLECTION TO SEE IF I CAN FIGURE IT OUT BEFORE SHE GETS BACK.

WE'RE PLANNING ON HEADING OUT TOWARDS FAIRWEATHER TODAY, WHICH IS A COOL MARKET SETTLEMENT TUCKED AWAY

IN A CLEARING IN THE FOREST. IT MIGHT TAKE A COUPLE OF DAYS TO GET THERE, SO SHE WANTS TO GET GOING AS SOON AS SHE GETS BACK. I THINK WE ARE MEETING A FRIEND OF HERS THERE, AND HE IS LEAVING FAIRWEATHER SOON.

SHE WON'T TELL ME WHO THIS FRIEND IS THOUGH: MAYBE HE'S GOING TO HELP ME OUT WITH MY HEALING JOURNEY.

IT'S AVIE'S FAVOURITE PLACE TO BUY NEW INGREDIENTS FOR HER REMEDIES, AND SHE ALWAYS LETS ME PICK A NEW TOY OR TWO TO PUT INTO MY SATCHEL.

IT WAS IN ONE OF THOSE MARKETS THAT I GOT MY SATCHEL – I'D MADE SURE TO COLLECT LOTS OF NEW ITEMS THAT I COULD TRADE, AND AVIE LET ME KEEP SOME OF THE COOL ITEMS THAT PATIENTS PAID US WITH FOR OUR POTIONS.

LOTS OF THESE PEOPLE DIDN'T HAVE MONEY TO SPARE, SO WE ALWAYS ACCEPTED TRADES FOR THEM INSTEAD. THESE WERE ALWAYS REALLY COOL STUFF – MY FAVOURITE WAS A SMALL WOODEN BEAR THAT THIS BEAVER HAD HANDMADE FROM A NEARBY TREE BRANCH. I KEPT THAT ONE FOR AGES, UNTIL IT FELL OFF THE BACK OF OUR WAGON AT SOME POINT AND I DIDN'T

NOTICE. I MIGHT GET A NEW ONE WHEN WE GET THERE.

I'M HOPING WE BUMP INTO SOME MORE PEOPLE ON THE WAY TO FAIRWEATHER, I'VE NEARLY GOT ENOUGH STUFF SAVED UP TO TRADE FOR A NEW NOTEBOOK. THIS ONE I'M GOING TO USE AS MY NEW NOTEBOOK OF INGREDIENTS - AVIE IS ALWAYS ANNOYED AT ME FOR USING HERS.

I HOPE WE FIND SOME INTERESTING THINGS ON THE PATH THAT I CAN USE: AVIE WON'T LET ME KEEP ANYTHING THAT MIGHT BE USEFUL FOR REMEDIES, SO I HAVE TO HIDE THEM.

AVIE SHOULD BE BACK SOON AND THE WEASELS LOOK LIKE THEY ARE WAKING UP - I HAVE TO GO MAKE THEIR TEA!

SHE REMEMBERED THAT DAY WELL. IT WAS THE day that changed the course of her future, Wylas's future and risked destroying everything that she knew.

Ava had returned to the wagon to bind the leg of Miss Ash, the weasel that Wylas had mentioned in his journal. She laughed at the memory, remembering the animal complaining that Wylas had "poisoned me by giving us burdock tea, he should be ashamed of himself!". Wylas standing to the side with a sheepish smile.

The couple had left quickly after that, sent away with some pre-prepared salve to fight infection and instructions to keep the leg elevated whenever they could. She and Wylas had a discussion after this, where he made copious notes (in her notebook) on the correct tea to serve patients in the future. The burdock tea wasn't harmful to them, she was thankful for that at least, but definitely not treating their symptoms and with an unpleasant taste to boot.

It had taken longer than she'd hoped to begin the journey to Fairweather. The conversation between the two of them had lasted several hours, with Wylas taking the opportunity to ask as many questions as he wished, writing down every answer on the paper and adding to his increasingly bulging notebook. This had become a tradition between each patient, so he could start to build up his own almanack of items ready for his own journeys around the settlements. He'd borrow hers to read, but after some mishaps around the sap of a willow tree, it had become a purely supervised endeavour, much to the chagrin of Wylas.

They'd set off around midday, the time of day where the sun shone through the leaves that were grasping to the branches like birds preparing to soar. It was always Ava's favourite part of every day, missing the early morning dawn that shone into their eyes and the darkness that they couldn't write with at night.

The route was usually empty, scattered leaves and falling flowers throughout the seasons, eclipsed only by the charmed frost that clung to the branches during the darker months. She could count on one hand the amount of animals she could remember them encountering on this road, one that she had walked along since she was a kit.

But this day was different. As Wylas and Ava walked along the path; him gathering seeds and petals for the latest experimental remedy he was 'confident that it would work this time', she bent over to grab some elderflowers from the roots of the elder tree that had bloomed into life during the warmer months. It was beginning to get colder, the slightest touch of decay beginning on the side of its leaves. She studied the plant for a while, trying to think of a way that this decay could be used in a remedy. Maybe if she scraped it off and added it to a jar with some oil? She wasn't sure of what use that it would have, but potentially her old notebooks might have some information that could help. She could hear Wylas pulling plants behind her, muttering to himself about how he was going to use the different parts.

She heard it first. A small gasp coming from the direction where Ava knew Wylas was previously standing. A muffled crunch of leaves being crushed. Then, a faint cry.

"Please," it began, "I beg you, I need help".

She straightened her back as quickly as she was able, the fast motion sending twinges as the aged ache in her bones flashing up as if it were a friend there to remind me that she wasn't so young anymore.

At first, she thought that a tree had fallen, the shadow from it so great it towered over Wylas. After a moment, she realised that it was a figure standing there, having come out of the undergrowth to the side. It emerged from the shadows like a dark presence, shutting out the light through the leaves that Ava loved so much.

It was an Exiled.

"Mrs Blackleaf?"

A small voice threw her out of the memory surprisingly violently, the action jolting her forward and catching her breath. Grasping her chest, she looked at the doorway to see the young Lucy Morreland, a small pine marten kit. They were the child of an older couple, so were always coming over to get remedies for either parent.

Ava shook her head to get the last remnants of the memory out of it, as if the threads of the events of that day were infiltrating her fur, needing to be rid of them. She could tell the young kit was startled at her reaction, so she was quick to reassure them.

"Hi, Lucy", she started, putting the pile of letters on the chair as she stood, "Sorry, I wasn't expecting you today."

"Mother is ill again."

Ava stifled a sigh - Lucy was never the kind to elaborate without questioning further. Their mother also tended to be a bit of a hypochondriac, sending her child for remedies for all manner of things. But Lucy did know that.

"The normal or a more specific remedy?"

"Normal." Lucy was going to stop there but Ava shot her a look. "She's convinced that there is an eagle following us, and you have a remedy that can deter them."

Ava reached behind her to the shelf of basic remedies and teas, grabbing a small pouch of chamomile tea and handing it to Lucy. It wouldn't actually do anything, but they always seemed to work as a placebo. And that particular tea was good for more elderly animals.

"Thanks, Mrs Blackleaf."

Lucy grabbed the box and darted off into the forest. Ava stared after them for a while, noticing the excited run of the animal as they ran off towards the Morreland home. The low hiss of the dandelion leaves beginning to burn on the edge of the cauldron pulling her out of her trance. She walked back over to the cauldron, settling down for some more mixing and reading of Wylas's letters.

TWO DAYS UNTIL WINTER.

AXEL WAS HIS NAME.

HE LOOKED VERY UNWELL, WHITE LUMPS COVERED HIS SKIN SO MUCH THAT I WOULD HAVE THOUGHT THAT IT WAS HIS ACTUAL SKIN COLOUR, EXCEPT FOR THE SMALL PATCHES OF BROWN. OH, AND THE FACT THAT I'D NEVER SEEN A LUMPY WHITE HEDGEHOG. HE DIDN'T HAVE AS MANY QUILLS AS I REMEMBERED THEM HAVING, AND THE FEW THAT HE DID HAVE WERE FLOPPY AND

SEEMED LIKE THEY WERE SECONDS AWAY
FROM FALLING OFF. ONE PAW HAD A
SINGLE CLAW MISSING, BUT IT LOOKED LIKE
HE HAD CAUGHT IT ON SOMETHING AND IT
HAD RIPPED OUT, INSTEAD OF FALLING OFF
ON ITS OWN.

HE'D SURPRISED ME WHEN HE CAME OUT
THE UNDERGROWTH, I THINK AVIE THOUGHT
THAT I WAS SCARED WHEN I GASPED, SHE
STRAIGHTENED FROM WHERE SHE'D BEEN
COLLECTING THE WHITE FLOWERS SO
QUICKLY THAT I THOUGHT HER SPINE MIGHT
SNAP. I SHOULDN'T HAVE, AS AXEL ONLY
LOOKED SCARY AND SCARED, BUT I COULDN'T
STOP IT.

"WYLAS." AVIE SAID FROM BEHIND ME,
"COME HERE."

I TURNED AROUND TO LOOK AT HER: THE
LOOK ON HER FACE WAS LIKE WHEN I ONCE
DESTROYED AN ENTIRE DAY'S WORK ON A
REMEDY (WHICH WAS NOT MY FAULT), SO I
STOPPED BEFORE I EVEN REALLY STARTED. I
RAN OVER TO HER, LOOKING BEHIND AT
AXEL. HE JUST LOOKED MORE PANICKED AS
HE STARTED SEARCHING IN HIS POCKETS.

"PLEASE." HE BROUGHT OUT A HANDFUL
OF COINS, THE MOVEMENT HITTING ONE OF
THE LUMPS OFF. IT FLEW OFF AND WENT

OUT OF SIGHT OVER AXEL'S SHOULDER. I TRIED TO POINT IT OUT TO AVIE, BUT SHE WAS CONCENTRATING ON AXEL TOO MUCH TO NOTICE ME. I FOCUSED MY ATTENTION BACK AT HIM, MAKING SURE THAT I WAS LOOKING AT HIM AS INTENSELY AS SHE WAS - OBVIOUSLY TRYING TO FIGURE OUT WHAT WAS WRONG WITH HIM.

"I CAN PAY," HE CONTINUED, "WHATEVER YOU WANT. HELP-"

"I'M SORRY, SIR," AVIE STOPPED HIM TO SAY, "WE CANNOT HELP YOU. YOU'LL HAVE TO VISIT ANOTHER HEALER."

I WAS SHOCKED, LOOKING BETWEEN HER AND AXEL. AVIE NEVER SAID NO TO SOMEONE IN NEED.

"PLEASE," AXEL BEGGED, "I'VE BEEN TO ALL THE HEALERS IN THE AREA, THEY WON'T HELP."

"I'M SORRY," SHE REPLIED, TUGGING AT MY ARM AND TURNING AWAY FROM HIM, "WE NEED TO GO."

I TRIED TO ARGUE WITH HER, BUT HER HOLD WAS TOO TIGHT ON MY ARM, FEELING LIKE IT WAS GOING TO BRUISE. I LOOKED BACK AT AXEL AND SAW THAT HE WAS TRYING TO STUMBLE AFTER US, BUT THE WHITE BLOBS MEANT THAT IT WAS REALLY

DIFFICULT FOR HIM TO MOVE FAST AND WE
WERE MUCH QUICKER.

AVIE CONTINUED TUGGING MY ARM,
DRAGGING ME TOWARDS THE WAGON. THE
LOOK ON HER FACE MADE ME GET IN
IMMEDIATELY AND WE SET OFF, CONTINUING
UNTIL WE COULD NO LONGER SEE AXEL. WE
CARRIED ON DOWN THE PATH FOR A WHILE
AFTERWARDS TOO, AND WE DIDN'T STOP
UNTIL IT WAS DARK.

I'M WRITING THIS FROM THE WAGON
AFTER WE'D STOPPED FOR THE NIGHT – AVIE
SAID TO ME THAT IT'S IMPORTANT TO 'RECAP
THE EVENTS OF THE DAY' FOR MY TRAINING,
BUT I DON'T THINK SHE EXPECTED TODAY TO
GO THIS WAY.

I THINK I'M GOING TO ASK HER WHY WE
DIDN'T HELP AXEL. AVIE TOLD ME TO
ALWAYS HELP PEOPLE IN NEED, AND AXEL
WAS SOMEONE IN NEED.

IT'S GETTING DARK NOW, IT'S REALLY
HARD TO WRITE NOW. HOPEFULLY
TOMORROW IS A BIT LESS BUSY.

THE NIGHT THAT THEY HAD MET THE EXILED was when Wylas first asked her about the past. Why she didn't help the first one to turn up that day. She'd drilled into him about the need to always help those whenever we could from when he was small, but he had also been collecting the guild flyers whenever he saw. Evidently too young to fully comprehend what those meant, interested only in gathering extra paper for him to scrawl his ideas onto.

The time that Ava first encountered an Exiled one, she was just beginning her healing career with her mother. She'd just finished reading the last of the books, created her beginners almanack and was ready to show off her skills in her first clinic for their home-town of Atolea.

The clinic itself was run out of their family home, gifted to the family when they moved into the village many years before Ava was born. The main foyer of the house had been converted into a large hall, white curtained stations with simple wooden beds dotted around. During the week, these were moved aside to make space for their family activities, all except for a single bed that was kept in the corner for any emergency patients.

As the youngest of three, Ava was used to playing with the children of patients whilst her mother and elder brothers cared for both locals and residents who attended the weekly service. That year, she was finally old enough and trusted enough to start helping patients directly herself, though still under the guidance of her mother.

Clinic day started like any other - Ava's first patient was Johnt, a small Jay bird with a torn wing. She patched him up quickly, prescribing flight-rest and sending him off on his way. She wanted to tell her mother immediately, but with the queue to attend the clinic wrapping throughout the entire village, she knew there simply wasn't the time.

She was applying a lavender oil to soothe a fungal infection on the arm of Ol' Mister Brandy when the creature first burst into the clinic. The hum of voices, both from her family and the patients waiting to be seen, immediately stopped, the echo from the last words hanging loudly in the air.

Standing in the entranceway was an animal. It was so covered in cuts and bruises that she didn't recognise it at first, but she thought that it may have been a small vole. A single paw remained, the other one a bloody stump. It was almost hidden within its fur, jet black. A claw was missing, ripped out; a sure sign from the Guilds that everyone knew.

It stumbled for a moment and fell, the messy sound of blood splattering on the tile.

The silence was heavy, the sound of breathing from the patients and her family being the only thing that broke it. One girl began to cry silently, her eyes darting from one side of the room to the other, looking for a way out. No-one moved an inch, the discomfort evident on all of the faces around the clinic.

Ava saw the older animals looking intensely at the hole where the missing claw was, a look of recognition washing over their faces as they tried to shield their families

Her eldest brother hesitated, looking at their mother to silently ask what he should do about it. She gave him a slight shake of the head in response, turning back to look at the animal in the entranceway. Ava could see it open its mouth, but her mother stopped it before it could.

"You are not welcome here," she stated firmly, her words causing those waiting outside the clinic to start departing, turning off in any direction they could to get away, "We cannot treat you."

Those who were in the clinic shied up against the edges of the walls, trying to get as far as they could from this...thing.

"Please," it croaked, the noise coming out rough like it was scraping the creature's throat, "I need help."

There was no response from anyone inside the clinic, the slow drip of blood from his wounds falling from his prone figure. It flattened its palms on the floor and heaved itself up, the effort causing obvious pain.

"There are no other healers," it heaved, "Please-"

It stopped the last sentence as it doubled over in pain, as Ava's mother stepped forward.

"We do not treat Exiled."

From its doubled up stance, it looked up at her mother with such pain in her eyes that Ava nearly intervened, but she knew that if she tried to help, she risked causing her entire family to join the creature in its exile.

It seemed to be an age as the creature begged for help, with her mother just repeating the same phrase. The rest of the clinic did not say or do anything for the duration; even the small children seemed to understand the gravity of the situation.

The Exiled one was quieter and quieter in its pleas as time went on, the odd cry piercing through the silence as a scream. Eventually, Ava couldn't hear it at all, save for its noisy breathing. Then, not even that.

It was a few minutes after that before anyone moved. Her mother was the one to break the silence.

"Clinic is closed for the day, everyone. If you could exit as soon as possible."

There was a quiet agreement between the patients as everyone quickly and uniformly left the clinic, stepping over the body of the Exiled as it blocked the door. Ava hurriedly finished the patch for Mister Brandy, letting the finch exit following his wife. Soon, it was just the family there.

"Reece, please could you get the sheets." Her mother pointed to the corner where they were found. "Ava, please sanitise your paws and then see if there is anyone outside who needs our aid urgently. And close the door."

"But Mother, I want to help here-"

Ava stopped her protests quickly after seeing the look on her mother's face, and rushed over to the sink where she could clean off the muck from the last few patients. As she left the building, she tried to avoid the pool of blood that had accumulated beneath the creature's body, but there were already bloody paw prints extending out from where patients had tried and failed to do the same. She went to pull the door closed behind her, as she usually did, but realised that the Exile would make it impossible. Instead, she pulled the curtain they used in bad weather across the doorway, and turned to face the village.

The locals hadn't gone too far from the clinic when they left; there was already a queue leading from the town hall, a back-up clinic that she and her family often used when their own home wasn't available for whatever reason. They all looked expectantly at her.

Ava sighed: what a first day.

IT STARTED WITH MISTER BRANDY.

At first, no-one knew what was wrong. His claw started turning purple, then black. He cut himself on a knife preparing dinner, but it never healed. It grew and grew until he was unrecognisable even to his wife, dying almost a week after the Exiled came into the clinic. They didn't link it to the clinic until his daughter, who had taken him there, also began experiencing the same symptoms.

Soon, every creature that had stepped into the creature's blood, either with bare paws or claws, was sick, dying or dead. Those who had been lucky enough not to attend that day chose to leave the village as soon as it became apparent what had happened.

The illness was spreading, the blood of the sick

infecting those further. A quarantine was started around the village, imposed by her mother, ordering people to stay in their homes. The only ones moving around the village were Ava's mother and eldest brother, running from house to house trying to save those who were sick. An eerie silence descended, broken only by the screams of families as they realised there was nothing to save their loved ones. It was only those who she saw outside their homes, holding their heads in their hands.

One of these times was different though. There were no screams of anguish as both Mr and Mrs Tail-feather died in each others' arms. They lived on the outskirts of the village and would have escaped the spread of the virus in any other circumstances, but the kind Mr Tailfeather had turned up to help Ava on that first day, helping wash the blood off the dirty paws of the children who attended the clinic.

Their only remaining family was their kit, a boy named Wylas, who was too young to realise what was going on. He giggled happily in Ava's arms as they took him from his family home, fulfilling the promise that the family had made to his parents before their deaths to care for the child.

It was only a week later when Ava's own mother and brother started to show symptoms of the illness.

Ava had to look on helplessly with Wylas and the youngest brother Tiyr as the rest of her family clung on.

Reece died first, given the task of cleaning up the initial mess, so was exposed the most out of all of them. Not that they knew it at the time, but using the sheets to clean up the blood seemed to slow the illness spread in her family, but not prevent it entirely. By the time that he took his last breath, her mother had begun to experience more severe symptoms, preventing them from burying her brother and leaving her mother in quarantine.

There were not many villagers left; the majority either having left or slowly dying in their homes. The once bustling village's silence became a permanent fixture. Ava could not help - caring for Wylas and guiding away visitors taking up all of her time.

Soon after Reece died, Ava was called into her mother's room. She had been leaving food at the door, knocking and moving quickly away to prevent exposure. She'd return hours later to retrieve the tray, but it was often left untouched on the doorstep.

Today was different. The door was propped open; the bed pushed against the back wall to be as far away from the entrance as possible. Her mother laid there, her once ornate beaver carved bed - a gift from a grateful patient - hidden by mismatched pillows that she had organised with the last of her strength. In the bowl next to her were bloody rags, which she occasionally added to, after coughing through the one that she held into her hands.

Ava stood in the doorway, not clinging to her mother's arm as she wished. The distance was somehow more upsetting than the situation; it felt so far away, but was the closest that Ava had been to her in weeks.

"Ava," her mother croaked, a bloody coughing fit stopping her speech briefly, "Listen to me, please."

"Anything." Ava had to fight the urge to run up and grasp her mother's hand.

"You need to leave now. Take Wylas and leave with Tiyr now."

"But, what about you? We still need to bury Reece- "

"No."

Another coughing fit. Her mother continued.

"Atolea is doomed. Those still here will die soon, but I do not want that to be you."

"Mother, I can't do this without you!"

Her mother laughed, though it was a bittersweet laugh filled with pain.

"You know more than you realise. You need to continue our legacy, both you and Tiyr."

There was a heavy silence as Ava contemplated what this meant for her future. She had never known anything but Atolea, and she was new to this. To every-thing - caring for a child, healing others and working on her own. There was so much she still wanted to learn from her mother. But still, something stopped her from continuing the protest, and she just nodded, a knot in her throat. She turned to leave.

"Ava, before you go."

She paused.

"Always remember, my daughter. It was the Exiled who did this."

Ava nodded, shooting a quick smile in her moth-er's direction. She knew that this would be the last time she would see her. She left the room, closing the door with a soft click. Behind it, she could hear another coughing fit starting, the sound echoing around the house as she left to find her brother and new ward.

IT WAS THE REALISATION THAT TEARS WERE staining Wylas' fragile letters that took her out of the flashback this time. She moved the pile from her lap, reaching over to the embroidered handkerchiefs to dry her tears. They were one of the only things that she felt safe taking from her hometown, and were added to over the years as she taught Wylas the hobby. Her most treasured ones were from when he was first trying to learn, the too thick thread covering the fabric with abstract lines. She had one of her own from when she was the same age, though it was now worn away from use. This was the one she used most often - and was using now - with the memory of her mother patiently waiting for her to pick a colour to use for the first stitch.

After some time and a big cup of green tea, Ava settled down once again next to the cauldron, adding extra ingredients as necessary to the concoction and thinking back. The day they encountered the Exiled themselves was when she'd first told Wylas the story of how he came to be with her, but she still left some details out until he was old enough to process the horrors of what had happened that day.

There was only one letter left to read, and she knew exactly what it would say.

SECOND DAY OF WINTER

After leaving Axel, we carried on down the path like normal, ending up in Fairweather that day. Avie seemed to be feeling different today, more worried than usual and looking around a lot. I think she was sad about not helping Axel.

I wanted to go to the market immediately, but Avie dragged us in the direction of the food tent, where she let me get a treat while she looked around. She came back once I'd finished my apple, and she'd found Tiyr! I thought it was a really cool surprise to meet him there, but apparently this was the friend that she was meeting. He gave me a carved bear to replace the one that I had lost before, so I made sure to put it in my bag.

We all sat down on one of the tables with the grains we'd got for lunch and caught up with what Tiyr had been doing. He had treated the person that he'd left to go and treat, but he'd fallen in love with her so stayed! I think her name was Berry or something. She was at home with their two children, who I'm looking

FORWARD TO MEETING SOMEDAY. I THINK THEY WOULD BE MY COUSINS?

TIYR SURPRISED ME WITH A NEW NOTE-BOOK TOO, TO WRITE DOWN ALL OF MY CREATIONS IN, WITH MY NAME ENGRAVED INTO THE TOP. I WANTED TO WRITE IN IT IMMEDIATELY, BUT I HAD TO WAIT UNTIL WE HAD SOME MORE TIME (IT'S BEEN A BUSY FEW DAYS).

I DECIDED TO TALK TO AVIE AND TIYR AT THE SAME TIME ABOUT NOT HELPING AXEL. I DIDN'T WANT TO GET AVIE IN TROUBLE WITH HER BROTHER, BUT ONE OF THEM SHOULD KNOW THE ANSWER.

WE ALL SAT IN FRONT OF A FOOD STAND TO THE SIDE OF THE MARKET, SO I CHOSE TO ASK THEM THEN.

"TIYR, WE MET AN ANIMAL ON THE TRAIL WHO WAS REALLY SICK," I SAID TO HIM, AS HE WOULDN'T HAVE SEEN AXEL BEFORE, "AVIE DIDN'T WANT TO HELP HIM. WHAT WAS HE GOING TO DO TO US IF WE HELPED HIM?"

THEY BOTH STOPPED MOVING FOR A MOMENT, EXCHANGING A LOOK THAT I DIDN'T SEE BEFORE THEY BOTH DROPPED IT.

AVIE DRANK SOME OF HER TEA, SPILLING

A COUPLE OF DROPS ON THE TABLE AS SHE PUT THE CUP DOWN.

IT WAS THEN THAT THEY TOLD ME THE STORY OF THEIR PAST, WHEN TIYR WAS A LITTLE BIT OLDER THAN I AM NOW.

I KNEW THAT MY PARENTS HAD DIED WHEN I WAS A BABY, BUT AVIE HAD ALWAYS REFUSED TO TELL ME WHY.

"BUT WHY DIDN'T WE HELP AXEL?" I ASKED.

"WHO IS AXEL?" AVIE ASKED BACK.

"THE HEDGEHOG ON THE TRAIL."

TIYR AND AVIE EXCHANGED THE SAME LOOK THAT THEY HAD DONE BEFORE.

"YOU TALK TO HIM." TIYR SAID, STUFFING A SANDWICH IN HIS FACE.

AVIE LAUGHED THEN, REALISING WHERE I'D MADE A MISTAKE. TURNS OUT, AXEL WAS ACTUALLY AN EXILED ONE. I THOUGHT THAT I'D KNOW ONE WHEN I SAW IT, BUT I THOUGHT AN EXILED ONE WOULD LOOK SCARY AND DANGEROUS, BUT AXEL JUST LOOKED LIKE HE NEEDED HELP.

SHE THOUGHT THAT AXEL MIGHT BE THERE TO HURT US, WHICH IS WHY SHE DRAGGED US AWAY SO QUICKLY.

"BUT AXEL WASN'T THE ONE IN THE

STORY." I SAID, "AND THE EXILED ONE IN YOUR STORY DIDN'T MEAN TO HURT ANYONE."

AVIE LOOKED AT ME WITH A CONFUSED LOOK ON HER FACE.

"THE EXILED WHO CAME INTO YOUR VILLAGE," I SAID, "HE ONLY SPREAD THE SICKNESS BECAUSE YOU DIDN'T HELP HIM."

THERE WAS A PAUSE FROM BOTH OF THEM AS THEY DRANK THEIR TEA AND FINISHED OFF THEIR SANDWICHES. IT FELT LIKE AGES THAT THEY DIDN'T TALK, BOTH AVIE AND TIYR LOOKING AT EACH OTHER AS IF HAVING A SILENT CHAT.

"YOU'RE RIGHT."

AVA REMEMBERED ONCE AGAIN, WYLAS'S words ringing too true, the words and memories circling in her head on repeat. She'd always blamed the Exiled one that came into her village for everything, but if they had helped him... maybe this wouldn't have happened. Even with her experience since, she didn't know what illness could spread through blood contact - it was not something she'd come across before it burst into the clinic that day.

Ava's breath caught even now, just as they had the first time she'd had this revelation.

The Exiled ones were the only ones who had these severe infections and illnesses. Things that the healers weren't equipped to handle. Was that why the Guild forbade anyone to help the animals? For fear that the events that happened to her village happen again? She knew that her village wasn't the first to encounter them, and definitely wasn't the last.

Present day Ava knew this to be true - the many Exiled ones that they had encountered since were some of the most complicated cases in her healer journey. But past Ava was still trying to process that.

That same afternoon, the three of them started back on the path to where they had originally seen the Exiled. Ava just hoped that it wasn't too late, that they were able to save him.

It took a few days to get back to the same spot where they were before. As they turned the corner, Ava held her breath and tried to hear any noises that might distinguish the creature from the normal rustling noises.

She checked the bushes where they had seen him before. At first, she thought they had missed the spot, but saw the crushed grass still showing his footprints.

"You...you have returned."

Ava jumped at the sound, her breath seeming to stop for a moment. She nearly ran back to the wagon at that moment, getting as far away as she could. He was still here.

Axel - that Wylas had decided was the Exile's name - was sat slumped against the trunk of the elder tree that she had been picking the flowers from earlier that week. He'd obviously seen Ava picking them, but did not know the purpose of the petals. It was something that Wylas used to do when he was a child, trying to figure out what each of the different ingredients did. The memory almost brought her to tears, but she quickly shook them away.

The memory made Ava's stomach lighten, releasing the knots that she didn't even realise that had formed there. She was in the right place.

"We did," she said, stepping forward towards Axel. "I'm sorry. We can try to help."

The relief from Axel was palpable. He sank further into the flowers, the few sections of his face that were still visible showing his emotions further.

Ava and Tiyr both donned a pair of gloves woven from soft vines and she gestured for Wylas to do the same. Wylas stood back for the time being, as Ava had advised him to, on the way there. Even though Axel himself wasn't going to hurt them, the memory of the contagion from the last Exile the siblings had encountered was very present in their minds.

They both slowly approached Axel, and Ava could study the white pustules. Now that they were near, she could see the pain that they were causing, standing out against the blood and dirt stains covering Axel's face. They were smooth and looked at first like some form of white burdock flowers that always stuck onto Wylas' fur when he ran through an open meadow, but she knew that these were not these. They seemed to be taking the life energy out of him, slowly pulsating against Axel's skin. At a different angle, she swore that she could even see some legs underneath it.

She and Tiyr exchanged a look - she knew he'd never seen anything like this either. It looked nothing like the insects that her family used to raise behind the clinic.

Ava looked back at Axel, trying not to convey the hopelessness that she felt about not seeing a way forward in treatment. From her pocket, she took out her handkerchief, wetting it using the waterskin from her bag and starting to try to clean off some of the blood and dirt from Axel's face. The water didn't go far, the cloth staining quickly from countless layers of muck.

"The least we can do is get you cleaned up," she said to Axel, nodding to Tiyr to help Axel to his feet.

It took them all day to reach the nearby lake, with Axel's weak footsteps and Wylas's hesitancy on controlling the wagon. Ava took out the cloth again to continue cleaning his face, but he pushed her hand to the side softly.

"Can you help me into the water?"

Once Axel was soaked, he seemed to relax for the first time, the water seemingly to hold his whole body up. Ava sat back on the shore, her paws hanging over the edge of the bank. Next to her, Wylas got a small cup from the wagon to fill it up at the water's edge.

There was a brief pause for a few minutes as Ava and Tiyr tried to think of a treatment plan that would work for Axel. Could they get the creatures off him somehow? Was there a potion that Ava had which would kill them? Were they simply part of him? Was it possible to-

A scream broke their hushed conversation. Almost in unison, Ava could hear Wylas spluttering and the cup clattering to the ground.

Her head shot up, firstly in the direction of Wylas. He was raking a claw on his tongue, spitting out the water he'd started to swallow. Ava started to rise to her

feet to help him, but another scream pierced the air from Axel's direction.

Axel was in nearly the same position as before, but was looking in horror at a white blob that was now floating in the water. Looking closer, Ava realised that these were one of the pustules that had fallen off. Behind it, it seemed to leave some open wound, which was leaking blood and staining the water red.

"It-it hurts," Axel spoke through gritted teeth, his voice barely carrying from where he had been floating.

"Gross!" Wylas complained from the side, still spitting as much as his saliva would let him. He didn't seem to be hurt or choking, but Tiyr went over to help him.

"Wylas - there is a basket in the waggon." Ava shouted to Wylas, beginning to wade into the water, "We need something to put these in!"

"But, Avie, I-"

"Now, Wylas!"

He quickly returned with a tightly woven basket made out of reeds, handing it to Tiyr who started following her in to meet Axel.

Wylas sat back with a thump on a log by the shoreline, with a sour expression in his face. He sat there for a moment, watching the two meet Axel and start to collect the floating blobs that were now detaching from him in earnest. He pulled out the notebook that Tiyr had given him in Fairweather as well as a stick of charcoal, and began to scribble into it. The start of a great almanack that he could use in the future.

As they collected the pustules from the water, the legs that Ava had seen attached were now curled up towards its body, unmoving. The open wounds that it left behind were still bleeding, with Axel whimpering every time the disturbed water washed over them.

He needed to get out. Ava handed the basket to Tiyr to continue with collecting, before helping to prop up Axel and swim towards the shore.

It didn't take long to get Axel to the water's edge, and she now that she realised it was salt helping to keep him afloat. He sat, out of breath, on the bank, keeping his legs out of the water. He looked different now, as they could see the brown fur that had been covered for some time.

It took a few days for Axel's (who told them his real name: Rowan) wounds to heal, the insects' bite seeming to have an effect on the recovery. It bled for what felt like forever; every time that Ava changed the bandages, they were spotted with blood. Luckily the heavy bleeding seemed to staunch after an hour, and they were able to keep his energy up with foraged berries and various tea concoctions that Ava already owned.

Wylas was always eager to help, thrilled that they had gone back to Rowan in the first place. He was the first one to offer tea, helped hold bandages when Ava changed them, and sat in front of him as he told his stories.

Two days in was when Rowan told them his own story.

THE CAULDRON WAS BOILING; THE POTION was done.

Turning off the stove, Ava then put the letters carefully back in the satchel, placing it where it had sat on the shelf for years. She wanted to keep it safe for him, for when he returned.

It had been many years since she'd last seen Wylas in person. He had disappeared over the hill for his next adventure, many months ago, turning and waving at the last second to the jill he had raised him since he was a kit. She remembered hearing the faint shout of "Avie! I'll write!" shouted from that distant meadow. He kept his promise, letters arriving from various points throughout his adventures.

As she began spooning the mixture into jars to cool, she couldn't help but think back on that day. Wylas had listened intently at Rowan's feet, clutching a small carved bear that he often played with.

They learned that Rowan was a forager, spending his days gathering ingredients and trading them with other healers in the area. It was his life's work and he prided himself on finding the most sought-after parts of the rarest plants.

It was on one of these days that he had come across the insects, cutting down some tall grasses. At first, it was only the one small creature, but it latched onto his spines, just out of reach. He'd tried to scratch it off on the ground, but it only dug deeper in. It was just one, he thought, how bad could it be?

Soon, they were multiplying over his fur and back, leeching his body energy and growing larger and larger. He'd gone to a healers' camp for help, but it only resulted in losing a claw and being branded as an Exile. Ava and Wylas were the only ones who ever returned to help.

After that day in the salt lake, Rowan seemed to be getting better and better, even better than he felt before the infestation. He had more energy and helped to gather ingredients for remedies, some of which Ava had only read about in medicinal books.

Until a few weeks later that is. He suddenly seemed to feel worse, barely able to lift up a branch to retrieve some hidden ingredient. It was Wylas who first made the connection.

"Maybe it's to do with the bugs?" he'd asked.

They decided as a group to go back in search of these creatures, but together to prevent any massive reinfestation they might cause alone. Ava and Tiyr found them easily in the same large grasses and caught one in a makeshift trap, taking it back to the camp to investigate.

Tiyr was the first to discover how they could use them. He'd investigated the carcasses of the creatures and seen the fangs that were protruding out of the bottom of their bodies. The live one tried to bite onto him as he approached it, but he managed to entice it to bite a stick instead. Behind, it left a line of saliva trailing out of the puncture marks it made.

They didn't know it yet, but this saliva would be an ingredient for one of the best remedies that Ava and Wylas would make, seeming to heal and energise the sickest of patients that they had normally been unable to treat. Rowan found his energy returning back to himself with a simple potion containing it. Even Mrs Morreland seemed like a new person, needing to send Lucy for less remedies as the months wore on.

This was what she added to the dandelion tea once they were added to the jars, sealing them closed and adding her label to mark them as she always did.

For years, there was one thing that Ava could think - thank god we went back.

"Ava!"

She looked up out of the window of the wagon and smiled, seeing the all too familiar hedgehog, with now healthy brown fur and sharp spines covering his back.

Rowan had returned.

Threads of Time

STUART WAKEFIELD

In a village so small it could be mistaken for a mere sigh on the landscape, lived Talen, the weaver. His shop was an alchemy of colours, a kaleidoscope of threads converging and diverging in intricate patterns. Scrolls of lore said the loom was not just a machine but a map of destiny, and in the hands of a master like Talen, it could weave together more than just threads—it could weave the very fabric of reality. But even alchemists get lonely, and Talen was no exception.

The days cascaded in a rhythm as consistent as the tick-tock of a wall clock, each moment sewn to the next in a tapestry of predictability. Neighbours greeted him with the same pleasantries, traded the same loaves of bread and jars of honey for his woven wares. His fingers were well acquainted with the loom, each stroke pulling forth a new creation as easily as exhaling. Yet, despite the vibrancy of his weaves, his existence remained grey.

Talen could craft works that made old women weep and strong men ponder, but what his hands could shape, his life lacked. Relationships seemed a thread he could not grasp; they slipped through his fingers like water, leaving him yearning for something he couldn't define. His gift for pattern and design failed him in the labyrinth of human emotions. Love was an enigma, a complex pattern he couldn't decode. In weaving, each thread had its place, a purpose. In love, the threads tangled, broke, knotted in inexplicable ways.

Children in the village often peered curiously through the glass of his shop, their eyes widening at the otherworldly tapestries depicting mythical beasts and heavenly constellations. But their parents pulled them away, whispering that too much time by the loom could turn one's mind, that Talen was best admired from a distance—like a beautiful but poisonous flower.

So, Talen wove his days into nights, and his nights

into days, creating universes in cloth, but never stepping into one himself. His loom was his confidante, his silent companion. It knew his dreams and disappointments, each woven into the material like invisible ink, only to be seen by those who knew where to look.

And thus, the loom spun, and Talen wove, each thread intertwining with his quiet hopes and unspoken sorrows. But looms, like hearts, have their own secrets, waiting for the right hands to unravel them.

What Talen didn't know was that a mysterious traveller was making his way to the village, a man who walked as if he had been everywhere and nowhere, all at once. And in his possession was another loom, old as time itself, ornate and enigmatic, whispering stories only a true weaver could hear.

Talen was about to receive a gift that would unravel the tapestry of his solitary existence, stitch by delicate stitch. Sometimes, to find what is missing, one has to look beyond the threads of the known world, into the hauntingly beautiful tapestry of the unknown.

And in that realm, who knows what—or who— might be waiting?

THE DAY THE TRAVELLER ARRIVED, THE SKY wore a coat of many colours, as if it too were woven by Talen's hand. But unlike any tapestry Talen had crafted, the sky seemed to pulse, alive with unspoken mysteries. Children paused their games to look up, and even the village elders felt an unsettling ripple in their tea leaves.

The traveller walked into the village square as the clock tower struck noon. He was an enigma, wrapped in a cloak spun from darkness and starlight, carrying a sense of timelessness that whispered of tales yet untold. He moved with a grace that suggested he had walked on cobblestones and clouds, through meadows and mazes, and perhaps even beyond the veil of life and death.

He approached Talen's shop like a moth to a flame —drawn not by the light, but by something deeper, a call that resonated in the very threads of his being.

"Good day, Talen the Weaver," the traveller greeted, his voice like a forgotten melody.

"Good day," Talen replied cautiously. "You seem to know my name, but I don't believe we've met."

The corners of the traveller's eyes crinkled as if he were smiling at a secret joke. "Names are curious things, aren't they? Sometimes, they find you even before you find yourself."

Unsettled but intrigued, Talen invited him in. The traveller's gaze fell upon the tapestries adorning the walls, and he nodded as though confirming something to himself.

"Your works are like a choir of threads, each singing a different note, but together creating a harmonious song," the traveller said, then paused. "Yet, I sense you seek something more, something even your gifted hands can't grasp."

Talen's eyes narrowed, wondering how this stranger could know the emptiness that often gnawed at him.

"Perhaps I have something that might interest you," the traveller continued, unravelling a cloth to reveal an ancient loom. It was unlike any Talen had seen, fashioned from a wood that seemed to dance with internal flames and shimmer like twilight. The heddles and the shuttle were adorned with mysterious runes, whispering secrets to those who would listen.

"This loom," the traveller began, "is older than both of us, older perhaps than this village. It's woven tapestries for kings and paupers, saints and sinners. And now, it's your turn to discover its secrets."

"Why would you give me something so...priceless?" Talen asked, a knot of incredulity and hope tightening in his chest.

"Because, Talen, you are a true weaver," said the traveller. "And a true weaver doesn't just craft tapestries; he weaves the strands of destiny, the threads of time itself. This loom will teach you how."

Talen felt as if he were on the edge of an abyss, peering into the fathomless unknown. With trembling hands, he accepted the loom.

"As the wheel turns, so does the loom of fate," the traveller said cryptically, taking his leave. His exit was as mysterious as his arrival, and before Talen could blink, the traveller had vanished, leaving behind nothing but a whisper in the wind and the enigmatic loom.

Left alone in his shop, with the ancient loom now occupying a sacred space, Talen felt a mixture of trepidation and excitement coil within him. As he touched the loom's intricately carved surface, he felt a surge of energy—like the first drop of rain heralding a storm.

For the first time in years, the predictable pattern of his life seemed ready to unravel, pulling him into a labyrinth of unknown threads and unforeseen turns. And in that moment, Talen understood that he wasn't just a weaver of threads, but perhaps a weaver of something far greater.

With a deep breath, he prepared to weave on the loom that promised to unlock the secrets of time, love, and destiny. And who knows what else?

The loom sat in Talen's shop like a well-kept secret, a riddle enshrouded in carved wood and ancient patterns. Night had fallen, and the world outside was a silent symphony of stars and shadows. Talen sat before the loom, an orchestra conductor poised before a cosmic score, and his fingers itched with anticipation.

With a deep breath, he took the first threads—rich blues like twilight skies, warm reds like heartbeats, and shimmering golds like rays of elusive hope—and began to weave. The loom responded as though it had been waiting for him, its gears and heddles moving with a fluidity that defied its age.

As the shuttle danced through the warp and weft, Talen felt a warmth, a sense of connection he had never felt before. And then, as the threads began to form their initial patterns, he saw it: a fleeting vision of another young man, his fingers also working a loom. The backdrop was different, the room steeped in the glow of oil lamps, the air tinged with the scent of a world long past.

Talen paused, his hands hovering above the loom as he looked around his shop. Was it a trick of the light? An illusion borne from exhaustion or longing?

He shook his head, convinced his imagination was playing games with him. But when he resumed weaving, the vision returned, clearer this time.

The young man—Kalen, he somehow knew—looked up and locked eyes with Talen for a heartbeat, a moment stretched across time, and recognition dawned. Both men pulled back from their looms simultaneously, each rattled, each questioning the reality of their senses.

Tale's heart pounded in a rhythm that seemed to echo through the loom itself. For years, he had believed the loom was a solitary endeavour, a dialogue between thread and weaver. But now, the loom felt like a bridge, a passage connecting him to another soul.

For a long time, Talen sat still, contemplating what he had seen and felt. Then, with a resolve solidifying in his chest, he returned to the loom. If this mysterious link was a thread woven by fate, then he would follow it, unravel its mysteries and complexities. For the first time in his life, he felt like an explorer stepping onto uncharted lands, guided by the North Star of his own longing.

Carefully, deliberately, Talen began to weave again, and the loom came alive as if fuelled by his newfound determination. The vision of Kalen returned, but now it lingered, no longer a fleeting apparition but a steady presence.

And so, they wove, two souls separated by the sands of time yet connected by the threads of destiny. Patterns emerged, symmetrical yet fluid, as if their looms were composing a shared song, a melody known only to them.

As Talen's threads intertwined with imagined yet vivid threads of Kalen's own making, he realised they were crafting more than just fabric. They were weaving a language, a form of silent communication. Each thread was a word, each pattern a sentence, and each tapestry a chapter in a story that transcended time.

Talen felt the void within him begin to fill, stitched together by the colourful threads of an extraordinary connection. His life had been a solitary tapestry, beautiful yet incomplete. But now, he sensed another weaver pulling threads on the other side, filling in the gaps, making the picture whole.

In that quiet room, where night met dawn and the past brushed fingertips with the present, Talen and Kalen wove tales into threads and threads into tales, each feeling as if they were finally part of a story grander than themselves. And as their shuttles danced in synchronised movements, they both sensed that they had just turned the first page of a narrative neither could ever have dreamed of—but one they were destined to tell together.

FOR THE LONGEST TIME, TALEN AND KALEN communicated through the unspoken language of their looms. Each pattern, each swirl of colour became a sentence in a dialogue without words. But as the days stretched into nights, Talen felt an unyielding curiosity, a thirst that couldn't be quenched by threads and visions.

Sitting before the ancient loom that had opened doors to untold realms, Talen took a deep breath. A sense of reverence fell over him as he prepared to do something he'd never tried before. With intent, he took strands of silver and gold and began weaving them into the fabric, each movement precise and deliberate. As the shuttle moved, he whispered softly, "Can you hear me?"

The loom vibrated subtly, as if resonating with his spoken words. He paused, holding his breath, and in that silent anticipation, the vision of Kalen solidified.

For a moment, Talen could see him clearly, as though the veil of time had grown thin. Kalen was staring at his own loom, visibly stunned, then looked up and met Talen's gaze.

"Yes," Kalen whispered, his voice a distant echo yet clear as crystal, "I can hear you."

For a moment, both weavers were immobilised by the sheer wonder and improbability of it all. The shock of hearing and being heard stretched between them, filling the space with an electric charge. Finally, the tension broke, and Talen found his voice again.

"Who are you?" Talen asked, his fingers unconsciously touching the threads as if they could bridge the gap between them.

"I am Kalen," came the response, "a weaver from a time long before your own. And you are?"

"Talen," he said, almost laughing at the symmetry of their names, "a weaver of this age."

A pause followed, laden with the gravity of their unique situation. "How is this possible?" Kalen finally asked.

Talen thought for a moment. "I don't know. This loom is older than time, given to me by a traveller. It has...magic, I believe. And a desire to connect threads that stretch beyond the physical weave."

Kalen nodded, a smile breaking through his initial

reserve. "I, too, received my loom from a figure shrouded in mystery, as if destiny had penned it so. And the moment I began to weave, I felt a pull, a call beyond the strands."

Both men looked at their respective looms, these ancient, mystical machines that had linked their lives in a way neither could have imagined.

"Then we are bound by more than just thread," Talen mused, "we are bound by fate, stitched together across the seams of time."

Kalen's eyes shone brightly, as if lit by a newfound sense of wonder. "And what shall we do with this tapestry of time and fate that stretches between us?"

Talen felt a warmth bloom in his chest, an ember of connection that had long been absent from his life. "We explore. We discover. We weave, not just with our hands, but with our hearts. We create a narrative that defies the boundaries of time and space."

"A tale of two weavers," Kalen said, his voice tinged with awe, "finding love across the loom of destiny."

Both weavers returned to their looms, this time with a renewed sense of purpose. As they began to weave again, each movement was a shared secret, each pattern a love letter, each thread a promise stretched across ages.

And so, in the sanctity of their woven worlds, Talen and Kalen began a new tapestry. It was a love story unlike any other, spun from the threads of dreams and draped over the loom of eternity, where every stitch was a word and every colour an emotion.

In this realm beyond the confines of time, two hearts found their missing threads and began weaving a tapestry that was, at long last, complete.

AS THE DAYS TURNED INTO A DANCE OF LIGHT and shadow, Talen and Kalen continued their unique dialogue. The loom had become their meeting place, their sanctuary. With each new tapestry, they revealed layers of themselves, unfurling like scrolls of hidden script.

Talen wove the tale of his life in a quiet village where everybody knew everybody else's name, but nobody knew his secret. With each stitch, he crafted the hills and valleys of his home, the cobbled streets, the changing seasons. Yet, amidst the bucolic scenes, he threaded in sombre hues, tight knots of isolation, loops that circled inwards but never out. His shuttle danced as he told of a life where love dared not speak its name, where his heart could not find its counterpart, and where acceptance was conditional.

Across the time-forged gap, Kalen's vision resonated with Talen's tapestry. With aged but agile hands, he began to craft his response, setting his own life into woven form. His world was one of castles and feudal systems, a society rigid in its norms, gilded in tradition but tarnished by prejudice. Kalen's tapestry showed great halls and chandeliers, yet in the corners, he embroidered hidden alcoves, shadowy spaces where he'd steal forbidden glances, where whispered conversations with other men took place but never lasted.

The dark threads meandered through both their works like underground rivers, surfacing briefly to catch the light before diving back into the depths. With every shared tapestry, Talen and Kalen unearthed striking similarities, patterns that aligned despite the epochs separating them. Both lived under the weight of societal expectations, both loved in ways that their worlds considered transgressive, and both carried the solitude that comes with holding a secret too long.

The loom became their confessional, a space where they could be heard and understood without judgment. As the threads of their stories intertwined, so too did their souls. Each understood the other's language of hidden glances, coded words, and the endless wait for a world more accepting. The absence of acceptance in their respective times rendered their connection even more poignant, as if they were stars that had been waiting for eons to align.

In one particularly intimate tapestry, Talen wove in a moonlit sky, each star a beacon, a wish for understanding. Below it, he crafted two figures, almost touching but separated by a void. The void was dark but sprinkled with flecks of gold—glimmers of hope, embers of a love that could be but had not yet found its form.

Kalen received this tapestry of night and longing, and for the first time, words failed him. Instead, he sat before his loom and wove a sunrise, brilliant and warm, casting away shadows. Below it, he replicated the two figures, this time touching, their outlines merging into a single form. They were still separated by time, but united in a future they could both envision, illuminated by the first light of a sun yet to rise.

As they exchanged these final tapestries, an unspoken vow settled between them. They would continue to weave, continue to hope, continue to love, in defiance of the worlds that sought to hold them apart. For in each other, they had found not just a confidant, but a kindred spirit—a love that time itself could not unravel.

They were weavers, not just of threads, but of dreams and futures. And though the loom that connected them was ancient, the love it wove was as new as dawn, as timeless as the night sky, and as enduring as the threads of destiny that had brought them together.

DAYS UNFURLED INTO WEEKS, AND THE rhythmic click-clack of the loom became a meditative chant for both Talen and Kalen. It was a rhythm that spoke of more than just the process of weaving; it was the beating of two hearts resonating across the void of time.

In that woven dialogue, Talen crafted the quiet moments of his life, filling the tapestry with intricate details—patterns resembling his small victories, the comforting smile of a friend, or the soft hues of a setting sun on an otherwise gloomy day. There were pockets of brightness in his story, moments where he'd found a semblance of peace within himself, despite society's unspoken judgment.

In return, Kalen created tapestries that sung hymns of his own quiet triumphs: the clandestine meetings with likeminded souls, stolen kisses in castle corridors, and the secret literature of forbidden love that he'd once found hidden in the back of an ancient library. Each thread was a symbol of resistance, each pattern a small act of rebellion.

Though the tapestries they sent each other were different in setting and context, the emotions they conveyed were remarkably similar, the looms translating, converting the specifics of their lives into the universal language of human experience.

Solace emerged in these shared tapestries. Talen saw his own struggles reflected in Kalen's stories of hardship and resistance; his own dreams mirrored in Kalen's aspirations. The realisation that they were not alone in their fears and desires brought them a comfort that neither had felt before. It was as if the loom had become a safe haven, a place where their souls could breathe freely and bask in the understanding and acceptance, they found in each other.

One evening, under a waxing moon that seemed to watch over him with quiet approval, Talen wove a tapestry infused with hope. He used shades of green to represent growth, renewal, and the life yet to come. A path was woven through it, winding yet continuous, leading to a horizon stitched in golden thread. It was an invitation, a beckoning towards a future he yearned to share.

When Kalen received this woven message, he responded with a tapestry that showcased a garden in full bloom, surrounded by walls but with a gate flung wide open. His threads told Talen of his own hopes for a world yet to come, a world where love would not need to hide in the shadows. The open gate was a shared dream, an understanding that while they were both confined by the limits of their respective times, their love had found a way to break free.

And so, within the walls of their secluded worlds, the two weavers found a sanctuary in each other. It was a space crafted from threads of understanding, knots of companionship, and patterns of love. As they wove their separate yet interlinked tapestries, their souls found the peace that had long eluded them, a peace born from the rarest form of understanding—that of one hidden heart recognising another.

In that silence, in those threads, they conversed as only true lovers can—in the language of shared solitude and mutual dreams. There, in the quiet sanctum of their looms, they held each other in an embrace that defied the boundaries of time, an embrace woven from the very threads of their being.

As days melded into nights and back into days again, the tapestries Talen and Kalen wove evolved into complex narratives of affection, as intricate as the feelings burgeoning within their souls. No longer confined to mere histories and chronicles of solitude, their looms now spun sagas of something purer, something as ancient as the threads of life themselves—love.

Talen started crafting tapestries that echoed the textures and colours he associated with Kalen—deep blues that spoke of timeless wisdom, radiant yellows reminiscent of unbounded joy, and intricate patterns that seemed to capture the very essence of Kalen's spirit. Each thread was a note in a love song, each weave a stanza in a romantic ode. His hands moved with newfound purpose, as if each motion brought him closer to bridging the insurmountable distance between them.

Kalen, in his timeless setting, mirrored the sentiment. He created landscapes of serene gardens, interlaced with paths that led to hidden alcoves where silhouettes of two figures could be seen. The figures were always together, standing close but never touching, as if even in this imagined world, he was mindful of the space that separated them. These landscapes were his love letters, his promises of affection woven in the fabric of time.

But it wasn't just their tapestries that were changing; the very act of weaving had transformed for them both. Every shuttle's throw was a whispered endearment, every pulled thread a caress, every completed row a step closer to the unattainable—physical closeness. The loom had ceased to be just a tool; it was a conduit for affection, each thread imbued with a love that was as real as it was impossible.

Then came the tapestry that would forever remain etched in their hearts. Talen, guided by a profound inspiration, chose to create a night sky tapestry once more. But unlike before, this night was not one of isolation; it was a night of unity. A single shooting star streaked across the tapestry, its tail illuminating the silhouettes of two figures standing together, their hands almost—but not quite—touching.

Kalen received this cosmic love letter, and for a long moment, he simply stared at it, lost in the silent poetry of its stitches. Then, with a resolve born of deep affection, he set about creating a dawn that chased away the night. As the sun climbed higher in his woven sky, the two figures were shown in an embrace, the first light casting golden hues over their entwined forms. It was the dawn after a long night, a promise of a new day.

Their looms were no longer just bridges that

spanned the divide of eras; they had become canvases upon which they painted their deepest desires and affections.

In their separate worlds, bound by the constraints of societal norms and the unfathomable chasm of time, Talen and Kalen had found something extraordinary. They had discovered a love as complex as the tapestries they wove, as enduring as the threads that bound them, and as inexplicable as the magic that first brought their worlds together.

And so, in the quiet corners of their different yet achingly similar worlds, Talen and Kalen continued to weave. With each passing day, their connection deepened, and their love story unfolded—one that defied logic, transcended time, and confirmed the ancient belief that true love, in any form, was the most potent magic of all.

IF DREAMS ARE THE LANGUAGE OF THE subconscious, then Talen and Kalen had become fluent in a dialect understood only by the two of them. As nights bled into the softness of their pillows, they found themselves wandering into shared dreamscapes, realms that seemed as tangible as the threads they wove by day.

In these nocturnal realms, the sensation of touch was both elusive and vivid—fleeting like mist yet as permanent as a seal on wax. Talen could feel the warmth of Kalen's smile, hear the timbre of his laughter, and sense the magnetic pull of his presence, even if they could not physically touch. And for Kalen, the sensation was mutual; he felt as though he were living within one of their woven tales, both a creator and a participant in a story yet to find its conclusion.

Their first shared dream took place in a meadow, bathed in the ethereal glow of a full moon. The sky was a blanket of woven constellations, each star a pinprick of the love and longing they had stitched into their tapestries. They conversed in this dream, not with words, for words were simply approximations of meaning, but with glances, expressions, and the shared language of two souls in resonance. They walked toward each other, and as they did, the distance that had seemed so vast and unbridgeable seemed to fold upon itself until they stood mere inches apart.

As they came close, reaching out to touch, they both woke up, each in his own world, the sensation of nearly touching still tingling in their fingertips.

This dream was followed by others, each a chapter

in an unfolding narrative. In one dream, they found themselves standing atop a cliff overlooking a sea of possibilities, the waves forming patterns that mimicked their woven works. In another, they wandered through an enchanted forest where the trees whispered secrets and riddles, each enigma a reflection of their own complex emotions and questions about their extraordinary relationship.

And as they dreamt, their waking selves were pulled ever closer to the loom. The dream experiences began to manifest in their tapestries, each woven story becoming richer, imbued with the energy and imagery of their dream encounters. The visions were so vivid that sometimes, upon waking, each would rush to his loom to capture the essence of the dream before it could fade, like morning dew under the sun's gaze.

Each dream seemed to fortify their connection, deepening the bond that had been spun between them. And each tapestry became a testament to these dream journeys—a diary of emotional landscapes, a cartography of the heart. The loom was no longer merely an instrument; it was an altar, a sacred space where the boundaries between reality and dreams, past and present, physical and metaphysical, seemed to blur and melt away.

As they wove and dreamt, Talen and Kalen knew

they were participating in a love story that defied defin-
ition, one that transcended the barriers of impossibil-
ity. In these shared dreams, they found a meeting point
—an astral rendezvous that allowed them a semblance
of the togetherness they both yearned for but could
never fully realize in their own timelines.

And so, within the interwoven realities of dreams
and waking life, they continued to build their own
world—a world where threads could sing, tapestries
could communicate, and love could bloom in the rich
soil of shared imagination and mutual understanding.
It was an extraordinary world, pieced together from
fragments of dreams and the enduring threads of love
—a world that only they could inhabit, if only in the
fleeting moments of sleep and the eternal embrace of
their woven tales.

ONE EVENING, AS BOTH LOOMS CLICKED AND
hummed in their separate worlds, Talen sensed a
change in the tapestry he received from Kalen. The
threads were tinged with melancholy, the patterns
knotted in complex swirls that resembled storm
clouds. There was a story within the weave, a tale that
held the weight of a thousand sorrows.

Curiosity gave way to empathy, and Talen set his own loom to craft a simple, comforting pattern—a visual embrace offering solace and an unspoken promise to listen. It was then that he felt the loom's magic hum softly, as if urging him to look closer, to understand the deeper story that lay enshrined in Kalen's tapestry.

That night, as sleep carried them both to their shared dreamscape, Kalen looked into Talen's eyes and began to unveil his hidden tale. He spoke of a love from his past, a man named Eolan who had been both a confidant and a companion. They had met in secret, away from prying eyes, hidden within the alcoves and shadowed chambers of a castle that held more secrets than it did occupants. Eolan was a poet, and his verses, like Kalen's tapestries, were coded messages of forbidden love.

However, in Kalen's time, such love was not merely frowned upon—it was outlawed, a crime punishable by exile or worse. Their secret was eventually discovered, betrayed by a fragment of a poem carelessly left behind. Eolan was captured and imprisoned, and despite all of Kalen's efforts, his love was executed, publicly shamed for the world to see.

Kalen paused, taking a moment to steady himself before continuing. "After that, I became a shadow, a whisper," he said. "I wove mourning into my tapestries, each thread a tear, each pattern a sigh. I vowed to never again allow my heart to become so vulnerably entwined."

Talen listened, his heart aching for the pain that Kalen had experienced. He understood now, the hesitance, the restraint that had underpinned Kalen's earlier weavings. Love, for Kalen, had once carried the steep price of tragedy.

"I reveal this to you," Kalen finally spoke, his voice tinged with a quiet resilience, "not to push you away, but to bring you closer into the fragile folds of my past, to better understand the tapestry of who I am."

As they stood in their dream-world, Talen took a step closer to Kalen. Though they could not touch, not really, the distance between them seemed to dissolve, filled by a newfound depth of understanding and an unspoken promise.

When Talen awoke, he went straight to his loom, his fingers guided by a clarity that only comes from facing the complexities of another's pain. His tapestry took form as a sunrise breaking the dark horizon, a hopeful light illuminating a storm-laden sky. Interwoven were verses, not of poems, but of visual emotions—a tribute to Eolan and an acknowledgment of Kalen's sorrow.

When Kalen received this new tapestry, he understood that his past, as heart-wrenching as it had been, had led him to this moment. Though separated by years and worlds, he and Talen had found a way to weave their vulnerabilities into a stronger, more complex fabric of love.

And so, the looms hummed on, each thread now woven with the full understanding of what it means to love with eyes wide open, embracing both the joys and the tragedies that paint the intricate, bittersweet tapestry of the human heart.

AS THE DAYS CONTINUED TO STRETCH AND fold like a tapestry being woven in the loom of time, Talen noticed that the atmosphere in his village had started to change. It was subtle at first—furtive glances thrown his way, whispers that hushed when he passed. But as time wore on, the undercurrent of suspicion grew more pronounced.

People talked. They spoke of Talen's sudden reclusiveness, of how he'd been spending less and less time in the market square showcasing his wares. The villagers muttered about the mysterious loom that had appeared in his workshop, an antique relic that none had seen but many had speculated upon. Whispers turned into rumours, rumours into theories, each more fanciful and malicious than the last.

Some said that Talen had made a pact with supernatural entities for his newfound skills, trading his soul for a loom that could spin otherworldly tales. Others whispered that he had fallen into madness, his tapestries the scrawled ramblings of a man unhinged. The most daring voices even began to question the nature of the man depicted in his tapestries, with queries that bore the sharp edges of intolerance and scrutiny.

Talen couldn't ignore the rumours any longer when one day, a small crowd gathered outside his workshop, their faces a mix of curiosity and judgment. With a heavy heart, he opened the door, bracing himself for the questions he knew would come.

The crowd entered cautiously, as if stepping into the lair of some mythical creature. They examined the loom, studied the tapestries—those intricate stories of love and longing—and cast furtive glances at Talen, as if trying to untangle the mystery by sheer will.

One voice broke the silence, a village elder named Margren, known for her stern disposition. "These tapestries, Talen. They are unlike anything you've woven before. And this loom—where did it come from? The village has a right to know."

Talen looked at the crowd, then at the loom, the silent keeper of his secret love, of his soul's most intricate weavings. He felt a protective surge, a desire to shield Kalen and their extraordinary connection from the prying eyes of a world unprepared to understand.

"It was a gift," Talen began cautiously, "from a passing traveller. The loom is old, yes, but it's just a loom. As for the tapestries, they are but stories—woven fables and dreams. They are my art, and art is allowed its freedom, is it not?"

Margren looked unconvinced, her eyes narrowing. "Art is one thing; dabbling in unknown magics is another. This village has always been a safe, tight-knit community. We can't afford to be entangled in unspeakable affairs."

Talen sighed. "There's no dark magic here, only the magic of creativity, of feeling deeply. If that makes me a recluse, or an enigma, then so be it. My tapestries harm no one."

The crowd dispersed slowly, their expressions still tinged with suspicion, but for the moment, appeased. Yet, as he closed the door behind them, Talen knew the whispers wouldn't end, that he had untangled only a single knot in a far more complex weave.

As he returned to his loom, Talen felt a sadness creep into his heart. How could he explain to them that this loom, these tapestries, were his connection to a love as real as it was impossible? That in a world bound by its own narrow perceptions, he had found a boundless freedom in his love for Kalen?

That night, as he wove his experiences into a tapestry tinged with shades of grey, he found solace in the thought that, even if the world never understood, even if his love for Kalen remained a mystery shrouded in whispers, it was real.

And in the loom's gentle hum, in the threads that danced at his fingertips, he felt Kalen's presence—steady, comforting, and enduring—proof that love, in all its complicated beauty, was the one truth that needed no justification.

DAYS TURNED INTO WEEKS, AND WITH EACH pass of the shuttle through the loom's warp, Talen noticed that something had started to unravel. It wasn't obvious at first—merely a subtle dimming, a waning sense of the magic that pulsed between the fibres. His tapestries to Kalen began to blur around the edges, the colours muddying, the messages tinged with confusion.

On the other side, in a different slice of time, Kalen felt it too. His loom, once so vibrant with the essence of another world, began to hum with a lower, sorrowful note. His fingers hesitated over the strings, each thread feeling frailer than before, as though the loom were a dying star, fading into the black emptiness of time and space.

One night, their shared dreamscape appeared fragmented, a jigsaw puzzle missing its key pieces. Their forms flickered, the imagery warped and distorted. "Something's wrong," Talen's voice echoed in the fractured space, his words followed by a grim silence.

"I feel it too," replied Kalen, his voice soaked in a quiet dread. "It's as if the strings that bind us are fraying, as if this miracle is coming to an end."

"Can we fix it?" Talen's words came out as a desperate whisper, a plea floating in the darkness. "I can't bear the thought of losing this—losing you."

Kalen paused; his ethereal eyes locked onto Talen's. "I don't know. Time has always been the weaver, and we but the threads. Perhaps it's decided that our time is up."

"Then we must convince it otherwise," Talen

STUART WAKEFIELD

insisted. "We've built something here, something beautiful and sacred. That has to count for something."

But even as he spoke, the dream started to dissolve. "Hold on, Talen," Kalen murmured, as if trying to stitch the unravelling seams with his voice. "Hold on."

And then Talen woke up, alone, the first light of dawn sneaking through his window blinds. The loom sat in the corner; its once vibrant aura reduced to a feeble glimmer. He approached it with hesitant steps, touching the wood and threads as if they were fragile bones of a long-extinct creature.

He noticed a piece of parchment beside the loom, weathered and aged. Picking it up, he read the inscription: "For true weavers, the loom shall unveil secrets, but even secrets have their season."

Talen looked at the words, then at the loom, understanding the price of their extraordinary love. Time, it seemed, was not a thread that could be cut or knotted at will; it ran its course, indifferent to the hearts it entangled along the way.

With a heaviness in his chest, he sat at the loom and began to weave—a tapestry filled with hues of desperation and longing, a visual sonnet, a prayer, to whatever magic still clung to those ancient fibres.

And as he wove, he hoped against hope that somewhere, in another slice of time, Kalen was doing the same. For if love could be woven into the very fabric of the universe, then perhaps, just perhaps, it could mend what was starting to break.

IN A WORLD PUNCTUATED BY THE RIGID markers of hours and days, Talen sat before his loom, its aging fibres fraught with an urgency that defied the limits of time. As he touched the warp and weft, he felt a pulse, faint but real, as if the loom itself acknowledged what needed to be done.

Simultaneously, in a time less bound by the ticking clock but equally chained by the unyielding hands of fate, Kalen stood before his own loom. His eyes were closed, his fingers resting lightly on the threads as if waiting for a divine signal.

And then it came—a flicker, a fleeting vision of Talen at his loom, eyes aflame with love and fear and hope.

Kalen opened his eyes. "It's time," he murmured, a whisper lost in the sea of unspoken words that stretched across the ages.

Back in his own time, Talen felt it too, a kindred whisper of intent, a go-ahead from a distant beacon. "Alright," he exhaled, "let's weave."

The looms began to move, threads dancing in harmony to the rhythm of two souls orchestrating their last symphony. Colours bled into one another, not out of muddiness but out of a desire to merge, to coalesce into a singular narrative. Here, a stroke of golden yellow from Talen met a dash of deep blue from Kalen, creating a vivid green—colours entwining to tell stories of meadows neither had seen but both could imagine.

They wove landscapes of places they'd never been, yet had visited countless times in shared dreams. Cities with buildings like glass needles, forests thick with enchanted oaks, oceans reflecting the kaleidoscope of dusk and dawn—each scenery a backdrop for the tale of two souls twined in love's enigma.

As the tapestries grew, they became less about individual stories and more about shared experiences. Less about me or you, and more about us. The fibres seemed to sing as they interlaced, harmonising in a chorus only two hearts in love could compose.

And finally, when the last thread was pulled through the shuttle, when the final knot was tied, both Talen and Kalen stepped back to behold their creation. It was magnificent, a woven universe that burst with a life of its own, a tapestry that told a love story between stitches and colours, between past and present.

"Is it enough?" Talen whispered to the loom, to the threads, to the air thick with anticipation. "Is it enough to bring our worlds together?"

In that moment, a shimmer radiated from both tapestries, a blinding burst of light that consumed both weavers and their looms. And then, as suddenly as it appeared, the light dimmed, leaving both men standing alone in their respective times, their looms silent and still.

But something had changed.

Though they couldn't see or touch each other, both Talen and Kalen felt a newfound weight in their tapestries—a sense of permanence, of a story etched into the very atoms of their worlds.

And in that weight, in that microscopic shift in the fabric of their realities, they understood. They may never hold each other, may never share a stolen kiss or a sunset walk, but their love, woven into the warp and weft of time and space, was now a part of both their worlds—indelible and everlasting.

For in weaving their final masterpiece, they had done what no loom, no thread, no tale had ever done: they'd spun a love so pure, so transcendent, that it defied the very laws that sought to keep them apart. And in doing so, they found their forever, not in days or years, but in a tapestry that told a love story without end.

As if the loom itself had whispered through the walls and windows of the village, a gathering began to form outside Talen's modest home. People arrived with no clear idea as to why they felt compelled to be there, yet they stood, faces alight with a curiosity that bordered on reverence.

Talen sensed their presence, and though he hesitated at first, something—perhaps the residual courage from his timeless love affair—prompted him to open his door and invite the villagers in.

"One more tale remains to be woven," he announced, his voice tinged with a confidence that surprised even him. "And I think it's one that should be shared."

They crowded into his workshop, young and old, sceptics and believers, their eyes widening at the sight of the ornate loom and the kaleidoscope tapestry that adorned it. Talen took his position, his hands hovering over the threads as if about to conduct an orchestra.

And then he began.

The loom seemed to come alive, each thread

vibrating with the hum of a hidden world, each colour pulsing like a beating heart. As the shuttle moved back and forth, images began to form, a narrative unfolding in woven syntax and chromatic semantics.

Talen didn't need to explain the tale it told; the tapestry did that on its own. It spoke of love and loss, of courage and surrender, of a connection so ethereal yet so palpably real that even the most hardened hearts felt themselves softening.

People gasped as they recognised the emotive landscapes, the allegorical cities, the mythical forests. They marvelled at the interplay of colours, how a splash of red from Talen's world met a smudge of grey from Kalen's, merging into a shade that defied description.

And then, as the final threads wove themselves into place, as the last strokes of colour completed the canvas, a shared sense of wonder settled over the room, heavy and sweet as the scent of rain-soaked earth.

"Is this...?" someone began, but the words trailed off, incomplete yet understood.

"Yes," Talen nodded. "It's love. A love story."

And for a long moment, the room was silent, as if the villagers were collectively holding their breath, afraid to disturb the fragile spell that bound them.

Finally, an elder spoke. "In all my years, I've never seen anything so beautiful, so... magical. You've brought something extraordinary into our lives, young man."

Others murmured their agreement, their eyes no longer filled with suspicion, but with awe and, perhaps, a tinge of envy. For in unveiling his tapestry, Talen had also woven a new narrative for himself, one of acceptance, even reverence, within his community.

As the villagers began to disperse, each carrying with them a fragment of the story, of the magic, Talen felt a warmth spread through him. It wasn't the same as having Kalen beside him, but it was something almost as precious—a sense of belonging, of being seen and understood, of love's transformative power.

He approached the loom one last time, his fingers gently caressing the threads as if saying goodbye. Then his eyes caught a glimmer, a tiny flicker of light that danced in the fibres, as if winking at him across time and space.

"Thank you," he whispered, and he knew, in that indefinable way of hearts and souls, that somewhere, in another slice of forever, Kalen had heard him.

And so, Talen lived on, his life forever altered, yet rooted in the same soil from which he had grown. He continued to weave, of course, but his tapestries were never the same, for they carried in them the irrevocable magic of a love story spun across the loom of time, a story that had become the very weft and warp of his being.

And sometimes, if you were very quiet, very still, you could hear it—the loom, humming its eternal song, a melody of love and longing, forever echoing in the spaces between yesterday, today, and all the tomorrows yet to come.

IN THE INSTANT THE LAST THREAD SETTLED into place, the loom erupted in a radiant surge of light that defied every law of physics and poetics alike. Talen closed his eyes, less out of fear and more out of reverence for what he felt was coming, a transmutation born from the alchemy of love and longing.

When he opened his eyes again, he was no longer in his workshop filled with onlookers. The room was similar, yet different, the air tinged with an aroma of distant spices and ancient wood. The loom in front of him looked like his own, but older, its wood marred with the soft indentations of prolonged use.

And there, standing before it, was Kalen.

For a moment, neither spoke. What words could capture the enormity of this communion, this sacred rupture in the fabric of their separate existences? They simply looked at each other, two souls recognising themselves in the eyes of the other.

Finally, Kalen broke the silence. "You're here," he whispered, as though saying it louder might shatter the fragile reality they now inhabited.

"I am," Talen replied, his voice tinged with awe.

Slowly, almost reverently, they moved toward each other, their steps a hesitant dance of uncertainty and yearning. And when they finally touched, when their hands met in a clasp that bridged worlds and lifetimes, it felt like the most natural thing in the universe.

The woven tapestry that hung behind them seemed to shimmer, as if applauding this climax to a story it had helped to tell. The colours pulsed brighter for an instant, imbuing the room with a celestial glow.

"Is this real?" Talen asked, his eyes searching Kalen's for confirmation.

"As real as the threads we've woven, as the love we've crafted," Kalen responded, his eyes radiant with a joy that eclipsed time itself.

They kissed then, a simple act, yet one imbued with the weight of ages, an affirmation that love, in its purest form, could transcend the very bounds of time and space.

As their lips parted, Kalen whispered, "I never thought I'd feel this, not again, not ever. But you've brought magic back into my life, Talen. You've made the loom sing songs I'd forgotten."

"And you've filled a void in my soul, one I didn't even know was there until I found you," Talen said softly, his eyes misty but unblinking. "You've made me whole, Kalen."

They stood there, hand in hand, two weavers from different epochs but from the same tapestry of yearning, their love now unbound from the spools of time.

Behind them, their looms sat silent but fulfilled, their mission complete. They were, after all, just tools —crafted by hands, guided by skill, and animated by magic. The true weaving, the unbreakable threads that laced through the very essence of their beings, had been the work of Talen and Kalen themselves.

And so, they began a new chapter, a new weave in a tale that defied endings. For love, they discovered, was the ultimate loom, a platform upon which destinies could be spun, re-spun, and knit together in patterns as complex and beautiful as life itself.

In that ageless instant, they understood that their story was far from over; in fact, it had only just begun. And what a story it would be, an everlasting narrative woven from the most timeless and enduring threads of all: love, hope, and the magic of finding one's other half in a tapestry spun across time.

Thus, they stood, the past and the present, two weavers entangled in the most intricate design of all, a design that could only be described as destiny.

IN THE QUIETUDE THAT FOLLOWED THEIR first, world-bending kiss, Talen and Kalen found themselves standing before their paired looms, each one humming softly, as though emitting a note of cosmic satisfaction.

Talen spoke first, "What do we do now? What tales shall we weave, now that we have bridged the unbridgeable?"

Kalen looked at him, his eyes warm with a light that felt like home. "We do what weavers have always done. We tell stories. Except our loom will now weave tales not just of yarn and colour, but of love—love that defies eras, defies prejudice, and yes, defies even death."

Talen felt a shiver of anticipation, like a story yet untold that quivers in the heart of every blank page. "We could be guardians of a new mythology. Our loom could be the birthplace of legends."

Kalen nodded. "Imagine the tales we could tell, the lives we could touch. Somewhere in some future or some past, there may be another Talen, another Kalen, who feels lost, confined by the world's narrow vision. Our tapestries could be their lifeline, a beacon guiding them toward their own impossible loves."

Talen looked at their looms, these magical machines that had spun their destinies so closely together. "But how do we ensure that the magic continues? How do we keep the loom from falling silent when we are no longer here to tend to it?"

Kalen smiled, a slow, heartfelt curling of lips that held millennia of wisdom. "Magic lives on when it is shared, when it is passed down like a well-loved story. Our loom becomes the heirloom of future weavers, each one adding their own threads, their own chapters to our ongoing tale."

"So, our love story doesn't end with us," Talen said, the idea settling around him like a comforting shawl. "It becomes part of a larger tapestry, an ever-expanding narrative of love and hope."

"Exactly," Kalen said, squeezing Talen's hand as if sealing a pact. "We won't just be weavers of cloth, but weavers of fate, spinning a yarn that others can follow through the labyrinth of their own lives."

And so, they began. Under their skilled hands, the loom sang a new song, one composed of equal parts past and present, tradition and innovation. As they wove, they felt their individual selves merging into a harmonious duet of intention and artistry, the warp and weft of their souls intertwining in an unending dance.

Each tapestry they crafted was imbued with their love, each thread saturated in the essence of their joined spirits. And as they worked, they felt the loom's magic amplify, its aura expanding in concentric circles that rippled through time and space.

Years passed, or perhaps they didn't; time was a concept that had lost its grip on the two lovers. They aged, but their love remained ageless, preserved in the myriad tapestries that adorned their sanctuary.

And when they were gone, as all mortals must eventually be, the loom remained, standing as a silent guardian of their legacy. Young hands took up the shuttle, eyes wide with wonder at the tapestries that adorned the walls, each one a chapter in a story that knew no end.

As the loom's shuttle moved once again, new threads interlacing with old, Talen and Kalen smiled from wherever they were, their love now an eternal part of the loom's never-ending tale.

For in the end, they had achieved their deepest wish—to weave a love so potent, so transcendent, that it shattered the barriers of time, opening doorways for countless souls yet to come, each one seeking their own pattern in the grand, interwoven tapestry of love and existence.

And so, the loom stood, neither ancient nor modern but timeless, its every thread a whisper, its every colour a promise, its every weave a testament to the enduring, transformative power of love.

The Ninth Secret

S. VALENTINE ASTORIA

The shadow comes at night.

The first night, a fresh chill settles as winter's fingertips reach down the roads from the woods, crisp frost cobwebbing the edges of windowpanes, misting the midnight air that burns the back of the tongue with each breath.

I lie awake thinking about my impending marriage. I think about Adelina and her brown eyes, her wide hips, her hair through my fingers as we lay on sun-dappled grass as couples do, on a spring that seems so long ago as to be a dream.

I feel nothing.

I think of Walter, the farrier's son, working shoes onto my cousin's gelding in the sunlight of a summer lost.

The chill settles, a precise blade under the skin.

A curious click of heeled boots stalks the streets, alongside the counterpoint rhythm of a cane on cobbles, but the view from the window tells me the streets are empty.

I sink back into bed and close my eyes.

The footsteps complete a lap around our house.

My head rests heavy on the pillow, but sleep has flown. My mother snores softly across the room, her pale hand hanging from the edge of the mattress, and with the way the shadows fall, I can almost imagine I see a hand reaching from beneath the bed, gently clasping her wrist.

The footsteps walk again, a full circle, and then silence. They do not retreat, they do not near.

THE SECOND NIGHT, I HEAR WHISPERS ON MY way home. Gossip with lowered eyes and turned faces, the familiar rhythm of a name I know. My cousin taken ill in the night, wasted, his skin clinging to his bones.

I hurry on.

My mother whimpers as I close the front door against the frost. The wind rattles the door in its frame behind me in protest of being denied. She sits by the fire with furs around her shoulders.

'I can't get warm,' she says between chattering teeth.

I brew her tea; it's all we have. As I kneel beside her, I stare into her dark eyes, darker than I remember, suddenly endless. The curled hand that clutches the blanket, lined with firelight, looks frail, withered, a dark welt spread down her wrist.

I reach out and she flinches before my fingers meet flesh, but even without touch I feel a terrible chill rising from her.

I smile, a contortion that takes all my effort. 'Don't worry,' I tell her, 'Soon I will be married, and we will never go hungry again.'

'I've always said... you will make such a good husband,' she murmurs, before she falls asleep.

Morning is heavier than I remember, thicker in the lungs. In a week, I will be married.

BY THE THIRD NIGHT, MY COUSIN'S BODY LIES swaddled in the undertaker's shed. It will be strange to stand with my betrothed at the altar without his stony face at my side, his gold rings catching sunlight, one absent, the one he paid to Adelina's father in exchange for her hand, and my salvation.

The price he would never let me forget.

The fog shrouds the low dark shapes of buildings in the blue early morning light as I sit by the window listening to my mother breathing. Her lungs have started rattling, so I stand vigil.

A scream echoes across the moor and my heart leaps, pounding hard against my ear drums for two beats, three, and then lulls.

Silence.

I see my betrothed after the funeral, standing listlessly outside the graveyard looking in, where fresh earth mounds atop my cousin's cooling bones. Her eyes sit sunken, bloodshot, in her narrow face, cheekbones stark, as white as her wedding dress. I'm not supposed to have seen it, but my mother is the seamstress.

Her gloved hands shake when I clasp them in my own. I kiss her on each cheek.

'It will be strange without him at your side,' she says, her glassy eyes skimming the strange monoliths robed with frosted moss and dead grass. The rosebud of rising cold on her throat looks like the whorl of a thumbprint.

'Wrong, somehow,' I add as I follow her gaze. 'It was his plan, for the family. Our family.'

Her focus returns to me with a flicker of tension along her jaw where a smile struggles to bud. My eyes travel down her neck where I see a bruise budding in the hollow meeting her shoulder in a strange ring, like teeth marks.

She tucks her scarf up around her ears and I look away. We depart in silence, but for the crackle of frost beneath our boots.

THE FOURTH NIGHT, I CANNOT KEEP MY EYES open long past the early fall of night and I awake in a silent house, in front of dwindling embers.

I start upright to a bang and a rush of cold that snuffs any warmth left within. The front door swings violently in its frame, open wide to the night, as a small maelstrom of leaves and dirt swirl away over the cobbles, following in a visitor's wake.

I close it and thunk the bolt home, my hands trembling. When I turn away, I jump. My mother stands by the stairs, her eyes unfocused and hollow.

'You startled me,' I say softly. She does not reply,

though her lips part as if she means to, and her shawl slips off her shoulders and whispers to the floor.

As I step closer, I notice blood pooling in the crevices of her collarbone.

I pick up her shawl and wrap it back around her shoulders.

ON THE FIFTH NIGHT, THE MOON'S PALE FACE absents the sky.

I mouth the name of God as I hear the stairs creak one by one as if beset with footsteps, blankets pulled over my head as my thumb traces His holiness.

'He who walketh in Light shall carry that Light, and shall never fear...'

The door to our room creaks open.

I hold my breath and despite myself, I glance.

The shadow, a darkness in the darkness, bows over my mother's bed and embraces her reverently.

A swathe of black falls over her face and I close my eyes to what is happening.

THE SIXTH NIGHT IS DIFFERENT.

Cracking the rhythm of unrest, I wake as if floating to the surface of a warm bath. My skin tingles with the lingering touch of a dream I had long forgotten to yearn for, and the air is sticky and sweet, as if I've tasted the breath of another.

Blinking, I feel the sweep of cloth falling from my skin as I sit.

My mother stands at the foot of my bed, darkness pooled in her eye sockets and her gaping mouth. She holds a hand towards me in a vicious claw, and it lingers between us, the unspoken recrimination. Guilt unfurls its ill blossoms in my chest.

The door behind her stands open to the creaking stairway.

She hangs over me until morning and I do not move.

THE SEVENTH NIGHT, I AWAKE WITH MY OWN tongue caught between my teeth in a rictus of agony. Blood burns dizzyingly at the back of my nose.

I sit straight up in bed. A knife twists between my shoulders. I choke on my breaths. I slump forward on myself, breathing short through the pain as cold trickles in waves down my spine and gathers in my gut, in my heels, in the grooves of my vertebrae.

When light finally, achingly, blesses me come morning, I twist desperately in the looking glass in search of the knot that pulls my shoulder blades tight, binding them together.

There is a handprint on my spine, long fingered and grey, the skin raw and blistered as I noted on my mother, as I noted on Adelina.

I am next.

I hold my hand over my breast and feel the heat of my heart holding firm and steady. Such heat blazes within against the bitter cold.

If this is what he craves, can I truly blame him?

It is only after I return to my room that I find my mother lies still under her blankets.

THE EIGHTH NIGHT, I STAND AT THE WINDOW I broke with my bare hand, now dripping red onto the floor, the handprint on my back holding me upright like a marionette's string. The night stretches before me like an unfulfilled promise, the cold slides into my bones like a lover into bed, familiar.

Footsteps circle the house as they did the first

night, moving eddies in the fog that now rises above rooftops.

My blood runs down the glass, beckoning.

My mother still lies under her blankets. The last offering for this winter, bar one.

I ARRIVE, WIDE AWAKE, ON THE NINTH NIGHT and I wait for him as he has waited for me.

I lift my head from the pillow, and I see the darker shadow standing in the doorway.

'Take me,' I say, prying open my shirt to reveal my throat, my fingers ghost-white in the moonlight that suddenly floods through the window. 'I don't want this life.'

The gold pinpoints glow like stars and a long silence stretches, then a deep rumble of an ancient voice replies, stone moving on stone, 'Would you like another?'

The moon washes over him and, from his shadow, picks shoulders, a slender neck, sharp features, plucking the strings of the night to shape a man from the monster. He moves like liquid as his hand reaches out, turned upward into the light in welcome, thin lips twisting into a smile.

I take it.

When he wraps me in his arms, his teeth find the last heat I hold, and I give it to him without misgiving. He pulls me tenderly against the jagged edges of his body. When I no longer know the cold, he kisses me with his bloodied mouth, and spring blossoms from winter at last.

Modern Woman

EMMA TURNER

« *Ses ailes sont coupées, puis elle se fait reprocher de ne pas savoir voler.* »

— *SIMONE DE BEAUVOIR*

They say the Modern Woman is not born but grown.

Like a willow tree, she grows best close to water, taking in every tear as fuel. She swallows her cries and allows the liquid to pool inside her, hardening like ice, until every one of her internal organs is encased in a glassy coldness. From this internal reservoir, she nourishes sprouts of warmth, bringing forth tiny seedlings that must grow to be great sequoias of success and ambition.

I want so desperately to be Her.

And so, when my fiancé says that he is leaving me and we are over, I do not cry.

I *want* to cry. I *want* to scream and cry and shout at the eternal injustice of it all. I want to demand that he explains himself – how *dare* he take my twenties and then decide I'm not the one for him? Doesn't he know these are my best years, the years of nearly every television sitcom show and new adult romance book? The years of boundless energy, promise and fertility? The years of finding myself have ended in finding myself without him.

I remember my mother telling me, before I was old enough to truly understand: "Never ask a man to stay. They're like wild animals; you can't cage them." She didn't say what women were. Were we kittens, sweet and docile curled up in the sun? Were we birds, bright and colourful but content to stay in an ornate cage?

So, I don't ask him to stay, my fiancé and partner of five years. Instead I ask, very carefully, very calmly, my voice barely shaking above a whisper: "Why? What changed?"

Henry looks at me, all honey-eyed pity and incredulity, as if surprised that I don't know. "You did."

He says I have put too much into my career. I have

not made enough time for *us*. I am not the girl he fell in love with. I am too aloof, I am cold, I have mood swings, I am unpredictable.

I tell him that he is unsupportive, that he is patronising, that he doesn't understand. I tell him I know that his job is hard but that's no reason to devalue me or mine.

He accuses me of not caring about our future or trying hard enough to make things work between us. I am sexless, I am absent, I am not there for him. "How do you ever expect us to have a future together – a family, even?" he demands, his hands splayed out at the obviousness of this question. "How do you expect to be a working mother when you can't even be a working girlfriend?"

It is strange, I think, that there is no such thing as a working father. There is only Man and whatever he chooses to do.

The words hover between us. Shards of ice suspended in mid-air, waiting to see how I will react.

Five years of following my fairy-tale love story from university sweethearts sharing a desk in the library to young professionals sharing a home. Five years of smiling and laughing at the same old stories and watching films I had no interest in. Five years of being available but not *too* available, of being affectionate but not clingy, of envisioning a future together but not scaring him away. Five years of putting him first, of packing my feelings into a backpack and carrying them with me, and of closing my eyes at the things I didn't like.

I was so close to having it all, too. The career, the house, and the maybe-husband-one-day.

But no. The Modern Woman does not beg for a man to stay, and she does not cry. Instead, I gather up my emotions in my clawed hands and force them down my throat. If I am to steal the Modern Woman's crown, I will need to build a centre as hard as iron and a voice as soft as the sky, and these sentiments are a deliciously nutritious blend of contradiction.

I swallow and then my words come out hard and steady. "Fine," I tell him – my now-ex fiancé. His eyes widen. He was expecting me to fight back, to apologise, to ask him to stay. At the very least, he expected tears. Instead, I send the shards of ice right back at him. "Fine, go. Pack your things, make your arrangements. We're done."

I side-step his jaw, fallen to the floor, and pull on my coat and my trainers before he can respond. "I'm going for a walk."

The front door closes behind me and the scratching in my stomach grows wilder. The unkempt emotions seize my lungs and for a moment I stand there on the doorstep under a cornflower sky, unable to catch a breath.

There is a woodland just a few minutes' walk from the centre of town, close to the river where we played as children. It was planted two centuries ago by a rich philanthropist as a 'green lung' for the town full of mills and factories, who otherwise spent their days breathing in dust and dirt and disease. I set off walking towards the tree canopies peeking out from atop the rows of houses and I think of it still serving that purpose all these hundreds of years later: a place to breathe away from normality.

Soon I am stepping into the dim green forest light. Either side of the dirt path, centuries-old trees rise from blankets of forget-me-nots and spread their verdant limbs up into the blue sky, creating a canopy of shimmering emerald and golden light. The earth is both soft and solid beneath my feet as I make my way along this winding path, passing dog walkers and hand-holding couples. After a while, I cross a narrow wooden bridge over the river, and I see it: a small break in the tree trunks. I glance over my shoulder. Certain that no-one is watching, I slip through the trees and enter a path that follows the stream deeper into the forest.

This path is mine and mine alone. Not even Henry knows about it. The gap in the trees revealed itself to me like a shining light when my mother died: a place I could be alone but for the birds and the worms, and shed my grief into the soil the way she taught me.

A little way along the banks of the river, there is a white willow. And at the base of the willow's trunk protrudes a small mound of earth, packed tight and marked only by a forked branch standing upright.

I kneel there at the base of the tree, and I begin to scratch at the damp earth with my bare hands. Soil buries itself under my fingernails and in the creases of my hands, but I dig and dig until I find the emotions hidden here on some other occasion.

And then I retch, and retch, until the ardour of feeling caught in my stomach and chest is laid bare there in the ditch, iridescent in the half-light, a pool of emotions.

I carefully scoop the earth back into the ditch, shoving and patting it into place until a small mound is visible once more. Then I push the tree branch back into place. It stands at an odd angle, sideways, questioning.

When I stand up, wiping my hands on my jeans and blinking tears from my eyes, my mind is as empty as my stomach. I feel more like the Modern Woman than ever before.

It is only when I get back to the front door that I realise that my engagement ring has gone, too, the sparkling diamond lost somewhere in the earth along with my awkward and odd-shaped emotions.

THEY SAY THE MODERN WOMAN IS FIERCE like a bramble, but sweet like the fruit she bears.

Already, one week later, new anger and despair is building up in my stomach. But I force it down all day after day and suffer the stomach-ache as I help pack my ex-fiancé's shirts into cardboard boxes while he divides up the kitchen appliances into *his* and *hers*. He is moving out as soon as possible.

Going into the office after a weekend of deconstructing five years of my life is a welcome relief, but now here I am, in another kind of endless negotiation.

I have worked in this office almost as long as I lived with my ex-fiancé, and in that time the number of young women in the team has barely shifted. I am still the only woman in the meeting room for our 4pm strategy planning meeting, and I am still the only person under thirty within a 20-desk radius. I think maybe the IT guy down the hall might be in his late twenties, and the girl on the reception desk is definitely younger than me too. But in most spaces I am the odd one out.

And this is what makes it difficult when I know that Keith, a colleague of extraordinary irritation, is wrong.

He has been talking – waffling – for about three solid minutes already, answering a question that no-one asked. It sounds a lot like he's making it up as he goes along, reciting 'hot takes' formed from only reading the titles of viral videos and using long words that (he thinks) make him sound smart.

Last week he caught me in the kitchen to ask how things were going. I told him I was busy, and he leaned against the fridge while he tried to give me advice on how to do the job I studied for four years to do. Standing with a carton of milk in my hand, I had no choice but to wait until he was finished.

I shake the memory from my mind. I could speak up this time. I *should* speak up. I have to say I disagree.

But how?

If I interrupt, I could respond more directly to the previous two minutes of rambling before he changes the subject, but I'll be labelled rude. Then again, Keith wouldn't think twice about cutting me off, and he's already hogged enough of this meeting agenda.

If I wait for him to finish, then I'll have to jump in quick – not *too* quick – before the conversation moves on. And then I will have to phrase my disagreement in such a way that doesn't appear to everyone else here that I am a) naïve, or b) arrogant, or c) hurting Keith's feelings. Do it too timidly, and I will be weak, ineffective, and meek. Do it too strongly and I will be aggressive, bossy, opinionated.

It is a hard balance to strike for the Modern Woman, and only She can get it right.

If I were a man, the worst anyone could say would be that I have a different point of view.

The meeting room is surrounded on three sides by glass: two glass walls, and a window. It is getting darker with every passing minute, the sky grey and clouded, and the view of the outside world is broken and veiled by the shimmering glare of the lights from inside the office. I lean back in my chair, distracted for a moment by the reflection of a young woman staring back at me. Pale skin, wide brown eyes, long hair scooped back into a neat bun at the back of her head.

Snippets of other unsolicited advice flash through my mind.

Don't wear your hair loose in the office – it will make you look younger. Pin it back, keep it neat.

Make an effort before you go to work. Wear a little make-up, mascara, maybe some lip gloss. People are more likely to listen to you if you look a little more polished.

Don't wear too much make-up to the office. You're here to work, not for a beauty contest.

Have you tried wearing heels? Maybe if you're as tall as all those men, they'll listen to you more.

Heels? Oh no, I haven't worn them since before I had my first little one – no point these days. But then again, I suppose you're young, you've still got time for these things.

Wear whatever you're most comfortable in; you'll do your best work if you feel confident in yourself.

Except that was never true, was it? Because if I wore something pretty to work, something that made me feel confident, and smoothed on a little lip gloss, Henry always got jealous. He'd tease *who's the lucky guy?* and make a point of mentioning that I rarely put lipstick on for our weekends together at home.

I narrow my eyes at the woman in the reflection. Does she look professional enough? Old enough? Young enough?

Finally, Keith seems to have stopped talking. There is barely any time left in the meeting; I have to say something *now*. I reach my hand in my pocket, feel the cool, reassuring solidity of a beach pebble nestled there, and wrap my fingers around it. *Be strong*.

I open my mouth. "I—"

My manager, chairing the meeting, spreads his hands. "Well, that all seems very comprehensive – though quite a lot to take in. We should probably send round a record of actions..." He scans the room then turns to look at me, and I think *finally, he did notice I wanted to speak*.

But I am, as usual, wrong. He smiles at me. "Would you mind sending round your notes?"

The young woman in the reflection looks shocked for a moment, her lips parted. *What notes?* I almost always take notes for my own purposes, and he knows this, but I have barely written a word since Keith started speaking and it is not my job to take minutes.

The girl in the reflection sits up straighter, draws her lips up into a forced smile. "Yes, yes, of course. I'll send them round later."

The room is filled with the sound of scraping chairs and rustling pages as the meeting ends. I wait until everyone has left the meeting room before I open a word document. It will be another late night at the office, and no-one will notice my efforts, but at least it's a distraction from everything else.

THEY SAY THE MODERN WOMAN IS NOT BORN, but carved.

Like a rough, muddy stone dropped into a stream, her edges are cleansed and smoothed by the rush of running words and expectations.

Every wrinkle in her skin must be smoothed, ironed flat, eradicated. She must not have a single sharp edge. She must be featureless, everything and nothing at once. She must not have the ability to hurt those who hurt her, but she must be hard enough to withstand their gnarled fingers pressing into her chest, her stomach, her cheeks, her lips.

She lies there in the darkness, feeling the fish pass her by, occasionally brushing by her with their writhing, dancing, joyful bodies. And one day she will be caught in the passion of the flowing water and carried along its course, swept out into the sea, and washed up onto a beach, where she will be scooped up, perhaps by her friends the birds, or perhaps by a small hand attracted to her glow among the sand.

And when she is at last scooped up, she will be as clean and strong and beautiful as a silver pebble, shining in the moonlight.

But I am not ready to be scooped up, scooped out by a child. Not yet, maybe not ever.

It is Friday evening, and I am trying to learn how to contour my face with the aid of a YouTube video, leaning over a mirror on the dressing table as I apply foundation, bronzer, highlighter, concealer. If I add just a little highlighter on the tip of my nose, the top of my cheekbones, the middle of my forehead, the YouTuber says, I can sculpt my own face into whatever shape I want. It is not deception – it is decoration, and decision, and self-determination.

The girl in the mirror stares back at me, unconvinced by the varying shades of peach and beige now blending their way across her/my face, and I think about how Henry leaving ought to be some kind of sign. It ought to be a chance for me to wipe the slate clean: to push away from the shore and sail out into the open ocean in search of something new.

Three and half years ago, Henry and I went to Redcar Beach, near his parents' house in North Yorkshire. It was early September, with the final wisps of summer sunshine still lingering, but the wind was cold and biting, and Henry wrapped his jacket around me. We were romantic, back then. We got lemon-topped ice creams on the seafront and walked along the pier, plotting how we could escape to the seaside to start our own teashop, and debating which ice cream flavours we would stock for customers.

Then we stepped down onto the beach, where the sand was covered in fragments of shells and strands of brown seaweed and slim pebbles that crunched and slid beneath our feet. I knelt down and scooped up something pale pink among the greys and yellows and blacks: an ovate shell, barely bigger than my thumbnail, delicate and perfectly formed.

I held it to my ear, then offered it to Henry. "Here. Listen to the secrets of the sea."

Henry only laughed. "You're not bringing that home with us, are you?"

The shell sits on my dressing table now, in a palm-sized decorative bowl my grandmother used to keep her rings. It reminds me that being carried in turbulent waters doesn't have to mean breaking.

I blink on mascara, then eyeliner, and eyeshadow in a shimmering pink the same shade as the shell.

Sexy, but not too promiscuous.

Beautiful, but not too vain.

The thing about appearances is that no matter what I do with concealer, whatever makeup I wear, however I do my hair, the first thing people will see is probably *woman*. For the Modern Woman, this is to her advantage. Her appearance is always flawless, but in a way that seems as though she has put no effort into it. She is the epitome of *I just woke up like this.* And so all of her first impressions are always good, strong, independent, yet approachable. She wears Woman like a crown rather than a wound.

But I do not – not yet, at least. And this is a current I cannot change, a river I cannot make flow upstream.

When my face is made up, I stand and walk over to the wardrobe. It is half empty. Henry's vacant shelves stare back at me as I take out a little black dress. I close the door, and my reflection shimmers back into view through the full-length mirror we attached to the wardrobe door by ourselves.

Have I changed since I met Henry – or even since he left? I run a hand across my skin, experimentally. Up my arms, across my collarbones, my narrow shoulders; down the centre of my chest, across my breasts, then follow the curve of my hips, down to my thighs, my legs. My skin is smooth, soft, flexible: I touch stretch marks on my thighs, and caress the folds of fat around my stomach, and I am reminded of my body's endless adaptability.

It feels good.

What if instead of being carried on the current I

could carve out my own path, rushing down hillsides and finding my way around every obstacle?

It is a silly thought. Heat rises to my cheeks and I pull my hand away, then step into the dress and zip it up fast, hiding the evidence.

One more dab of concealer under my eyes, and it is time to go out.

THEY SAY THE MODERN WOMAN IS FREE LIKE A bird, but more often caged.

I have not seen Beth for eight and a half months, but it is as if we never parted ways. Three weeks after the end of my relationship, we meet for brunch and coffee in town and talk in a ceaseless stream through mouthfuls of poached egg and avocado, then chatter as we wander through the shopping arcade and flip through shelves of second-hand books in charity shops. We trade travel stories and work complaints and TV reviews as we take a long, slow walk through the park, and by the time we loop back to the town centre again it is growing dark, but we are not tired and still have so much comfort to take in each other's company.

"Quick drink before I get the train back?" Beth suggests, and I nod. Suddenly I am too aware that despite nearly six hours of catching up, there are still so many things I have not told her. Things I have not told anyone. Things I can barely voice to myself.

Soon enough we are sitting in a darkened booth with a glass of Prosecco each. Beth insisted, saying it'd likely be another six months before we found another mutually beneficial space in our calendars, so we might as well celebrate anything coming up in advance. I couldn't think of any excuse to say no.

Now Beth sips from one glass and I stare at the other. I push the glass gently towards the centre of the table, trying to make it look like an absent-minded movement, staring into the rising bubbles as if they hold the answer to what I should do.

"Is everything okay?" Beth asks, after a long moment. "I mean, aside from the obvious, with Henry gone... Is there something else?"

It's not feminine intuition. She isn't psychic. She's just a good friend: observant, patient, perceptive.

"... I'm not sure," I say slowly. My heart starts to pound, fast, hard, as if I am about to run. I can feel a hot haze rushing to my cheeks. There's no going back now.

I don't know if I can say it *out loud*. There is a long silence, punctured only by the clatter of dishes in the kitchen and laughter from a group of guys a few tables away.

"Do you want to talk about it?" Beth asks, her head cocked to one side, her eyes slightly narrowed, listening, waiting, trying to understand.

"I think – I think I'm pregnant," I say, very quickly and very quietly. I say 'I think', as if three positive pregnancy tests have still left me with some element of uncertainty.

Beth's eyes widen. "Oh. *Oh.*" I see her eyes flicker to the untouched glass of Prosecco. "Sorry, I didn't – I never... I guess it's Henry's? Are you going to...?"

The question is unfinished but hangs in the air nevertheless: *Are you going to keep it?*

Already, it seems that questions about a potential baby come before questions about *me,* the potential mother. Funny how quickly priorities change.

"Sorry," Beth whispers, swallowing hard. "You don't have to answer that. How are you feeling?"

I shake my head. "I don't know. Confused. Nauseous. I don't know how it's even possible..."

Beth reaches over the table to place her hand over mine.

"I mean, we were careful... I've never even really wanted children – especially not like this, I mean, maybe if I found the right person... but Henry is gone and he definitely wasn't it." I'm rambling to stop myself crying. I swallow back the unwanted regret and bitterness. "We talked about it once, and I always said I wasn't sure... it feels like some cruel curse for it to happen now, on top of everything."

It's only speaking out loud that I realise the truth of it: it feels like a curse that just when I was so close to being *Her,* That Girl, the one who could have it all – I suddenly seem to have none of it at all. My life is messy in a way that the stories never seem to allow for.

"I don't know what I did to deserve this," I mumble. Was Henry right, after all – have I changed too much for the worse, lost myself in the pursuit of a myth? Did I work too hard, or not hard enough? Was I not pretty enough, or was it that I shouldn't have cared how I looked in the first place? Did I miss a step one too many times in my skincare ritual and anger the goddesses of collagen? Did I not work out consistently enough, did I eat too many ice creams, or did I get too lost in myself and forget about those around me? Or is this all some kind of test, and I'm supposed to rise to the challenge of being a single mother bravely without complaining?

"'This' doesn't have to be anything you don't want. You know you have choices," Beth says, very quietly, almost in a whisper. "And I'm here whatever you choose."

Choices. Something clicks open in my mind. Because of course I am not cursed. The very fact that I have options right now is proof of that – perhaps if I was sitting in a bar over the ocean somewhere, or if I fell back in time, not even very far away or long ago, I'd be staring into the face of a future I didn't choose, no control over my own body. The decision would have already been made by a man I'd never even met.

I forgot for a moment that we can pick up a pen to write the ending of this story, too.

I sit up straighter in my seat. The Modern Woman might be a mother, or she might not, but *I* do not want to be a mother, at least not right now. And for once I want to be the river, carving my own path, rather than the pebbles worn into smooth surfaces without meaning.

I look into my best friend's eyes and squeeze her hand back. "Thank you."

And then I reach for the Prosecco, to toast freedom and friendship and autonomy and choice.

T‍HEY SAY THE M‍ODERN W‍OMAN IS A changeling, always shifting shape.

All of the stories about her are a little bit different. Some tales are glossy, some are matte, some written in ink and others captured on film or passed down the generations. They overlap, twist together, clasp hands and then contradict each other. They break apart, they are brittle, they have clip-on accessories.

In almost every one of the stories, she is *successful:* she is a high-flying CEO, a leading actress, a politician or a selfless campaigner – all while still being kind, and a good mother, a good wife, a good friend and sister and daughter, *and* accepting less money than her male counterparts. As a result, I have thought for a long time that the first step in my path was to grow my own career. I put so much into my job, into my quest to be Her, that there was nothing left to offer myself – or the man who shared my bed.

But no more. Now I apply for jobs not because of how they might look, where they might lead, but because I want them. The job titles might not be so glamorous, and it's scary to be changing track. But the new story I'm telling myself is that the Modern Woman can't succeed unless she's happy.

Exactly five months since my life fell apart, I am

walking home from work when I get a phone call to say I have got a new job.

Just as when Henry told me he was leaving, I almost cry. Cry from joy, cry from fear, cry from relief. Cry from exhaustion because I have worked so hard to get here and every step up the ladder has been uphill agony.

The hiring manager on the other end of the phone is waiting for me to say something. Her name is Susan, and on the interview day she was wearing a periwinkle blouse that seemed to perfectly match her eyes. So coordinated, so put together, and so effortless – she probably wasn't even wearing makeup. I imagine these eyes staring at me as silence stretches out over the phone line. For a moment, I wonder if *she* is competing to be the next Modern Woman – if so, is she hiring me because she does not see me as a threat? Or perhaps empowering other woman is part of her strategy. *Kill them with kindness.*

But no. There is no competition. I am trying to stop listening to the stories, but it is hard, and sometimes the habit sticks fast.

"I…" I begin, but the words get stuck somewhere on the way out.

I have pushed on doors that were not open. I have stood up at the front of meeting rooms and presented over and over again until my voice did not wobble, and I no longer saw the patronising stares. I have made suggestions with smiling emojis and doggedly carried out every action from the meeting minutes until my eyes were red from the screen glare. I have taken notes at the whim of greying men and sat silently in meetings without anyone asking for my thoughts and racked my brain for answers to prove I have something to say. I have proven everyone wrong and never said 'I told you so'. I have been called naïve, told I must not preach, told I must be more ambitious, told I must be *less*.

None of it was right. Not for me. So yes, this is just a new job, but still I almost shed tears.

"Th- thank you," I murmur, when the joy has settled in my stomach. "It's such an honour to be chosen for the role. You won't regret it."

THEY SAY THE MODERN WOMAN IS NOT BORN, but burned.

Like a lone Oak in the midst of a forest fire, with charred skin but a beating heart. Alive in the midst of a burning planet, and still growing resolutely upwards. She is made resistant through the roots that form invisible networks beneath her feet and the mice that create new life in the hollows of her trunk. Perhaps she bleeds for a moment, perhaps she loses a limb in the storm, but she swears that the sacrifice of a part is only for the longevity of the whole.

It has been six months since Henry moved out and it is time to heal some of those neglected scars. I am back in the forest once more, autumn leaves beneath my feet and a cool breeze in my hair. The canopy above has slowly curled and twisted its way from bright green into muted umber and bronze, and now the soil is moist and slippery with the beginnings of a wet winter.

With each step forward, I think about my mother, whose favourite season was Autumn. She said for a long time that it was because it wasn't too cold, but it was cold enough to cover up; she would wear big baggy jumpers and long skirts, hiding away whatever terrible sins she felt were written in her wrinkles or the curve of her stomach.

I wished that she loved it for the same reasons I did: the end of Summer was also the beginning of something else. With the cool breeze comes a cooling and slowing of passions, along with spiced drinks and pumpkins and candlelight. Autumn has always like more of a beginning to me than Spring: Autumn is the season of the phoenix, rising from the ashes, and of freshly-picked apples and abundant harvests that will carry us through the winter.

The Modern Woman in the stories doesn't get to see the seasons like that and I pity her.

I take my usual detour from the path, winding my way through the trunks and along the riverbank until I reach my white willow. By way of greeting, she trails her remaining tresses, now a pale buttercup yellow, into the flowing stream.

I kneel next to the base of her trunk as I always do, and then dig my hands into the soft, damp mound of earth until I feel the sharp fragments of abandoned emotions within. I poke and cup and shape the mound into a new mouth: a teacup-shaped dip in the earth. Then I take out today's offering: a small white tea-light and a box of matches.

With all the care of a mother nursing a new-born, I place the tiny candle into the damp hole in the ground, then light it.

Instantly, the glow of the flame calms me.

Through the flickering orange heat of the candle, all of the ugly parts of myself, buried here over the course of years, start to melt – and then to evaporate. The scent of them is acrid, and for a moment I think I will retch again. My eyes sting and my throat burns and my nostrils sear with disgust, but I keep breathing, in and out, in and out, taking in every last drop.

Finally, the air turns sweet with vanilla and there is nothing left but the candle and the earth and the river and the trees.

"Thank you," I whisper. I lean forward and snuff the candle out.

I will never bury the ugly parts of myself underground again.

THEY SAY THE MODERN WOMAN CAN NEVER die, but she can drown.

The Modern Woman is a river flowing through a deep and gorgeous valley. She provides a path for clear water from the mountains to the sea. Glaciers melt into her; she becomes one with the ocean; she contains endless cycles, is endlessly cool.

Like a river, her forces stir up the soil of the riverbanks, sending nutrients spinning into her churning currents, bringing life and change to a whole ecosystem.

And also like a river, she carves up territories with snake-like borders, dividing man from man and drowning them when they forget her power. She can smash bridges and flood towns just as quickly as she can feed us all.

For years the story of the Modern Woman has led my life, carried me in directions I was told I should want and twisted my heart into shapes that hurt no-one but myself. I have tried to peel back her grip gently, and still she clings on. But there is one more story about her: a version where I can write the ending.

When I was a child, I loved water. I loved trips to the leisure centre for school swimming lessons and I loved summer holidays in Blackpool, where I could run between the sand and the sea all day while my mother laid on a beach towel flipping through magazines. Then came my teenage years and I became obsessed with those same magazines' advice on how to achieve a 'beach body' and I grew afraid to be seen in a swimming costume. I still loved the water, but it has been a long time since I felt comfortable in its embrace. Instead, I collect pebbles and shells and seek out secret riverside paths.

Further upstream from the river that meanders through the woodland and past my white willow, there is a waterfall where the water plunges over a cliff edge in one vast and thunderous torrent. Below the cascade, there is a pool, semi-circular, deep enough to dive into, and enclosed on all sides by rocks.

I have taken the day off work and gone for a long walk out of town and up to the waterfall. It is here that I am choosing to wash away the pages that have long stuck to my skin, clogged my pores and deafened my ears. I stand on the slick black rocks of the riverbank, just above the pool, and stare down at the churning waters below.

It has been raining for days and the water is deeper than usual, a little more turbulent, a little more beautiful. The duality – power *and* beauty, life *and* death – is clearer than ever in her depths. It is the perfect location to start afresh.

I take a step closer to the edge. I feel the rough stone beneath my bare feet, and I gulp in a deep, grounding breath. The twisting currents beckon me.

I jump.

Instantly, ice, everywhere. My limbs are frozen by it; I try to push outwards with my hands, my arms, my thighs, my ankles. I cannot feel if I am moving my own body or if my body is being merely swept along with the water, dragged down into some unseen undercurrent. The world is a blur of muddy green and brackish blue. I struggle upwards, and water flows into my mouth, my nose, my ears.

I am drowning.

This is how I will die, trying to wash the last of Her from me.

Strong hands grip my shoulders, and I feel someone or something tugging me down. I think: *She won't let me go.*

How fitting that I should die like this, dragged underwater by a myth, a final story, a final lie. She failed to starve me, to isolate me, to split me in two or work me into the ground – but she gets us all in the end.

No. The voice – my voice – rings clear in my mind. *I didn't come here to die. I came here to be free.*

I kick out harder, thrashing and writhing against the current that pulls me down. The water grows lighter. I feel a weight slip away.

Suddenly I am being pulled *upwards,* and there is air again, and I gasp and splutter and cough. My arms scrape against rock and my back hits something hard. I am lying down at the river's edge. My lungs burn. My eyes sting. My limbs shake in shock and cold.

"Are you okay?" someone demands. A female voice. "Breathe – can you breathe?" There are fingers on my wrist and neck, checking my pulse.

I cough again and manage to nod. "I'm alive," I rasp. The words are as much for my own benefit as theirs.

I blink furiously until my vision settles and my saviour comes into view. A woman in a dripping purple fleece and black leggings. Behind her, a man is holding a phone to his ear, speaking urgent words into the mouthpiece.

"Hold on, help is on the way," the woman urges. "It's been raining too much to swim out here today – didn't you see the signs?"

"I didn't see," I croak. A lie. I knew there was no getting out of this without risk, but the risk was worth it to be free. "Thank you – for saving me."

The words settle and I realise they aren't enough. I thought this was an ending I had to write alone – but how fitting that my saviour should be another woman. I reach out and grab her hand, squeezing weakly. "Really, *thank you*."

"The ambulance is on its way," the man calls over to us. "Hang on."

I nod numbly, and though my limbs ache and my throat is on fire, a quick scan of my body tells me I am going to be okay.

Because in my brush with death, I lost something. My skin is smooth again: gone are the scars of expectations, insult, and objectification.

As sirens wail in the distance, I feel *new*.

About the Authors

MIMI BROWN

Mimi Brown is originally from Hertfordshire. She works as a performer in the creative industries and is due to graduate soon from her degree in creative writing. She has participated in (and won) four NaNoWriMo events and enjoys work ranging from fantasy, to gothic, to sci-fi, to thriller, to historical. She has a soft spot for the merging of these genres to unearth something new. Other than prose writing, Mimi enjoys working as a lyricist and performer. And owls. Mimi always enjoys owls. Mimi can be followed on Instagram at @mimi.e.brown

TAYLOR MCLEOD

Taylor Mcleod is a legal professional by day and an avid writer by night. She lives in Hertfordshire with her partner and their house rabbit and entertains them both with her various writing projects. She began writing with The Hertfordshire Writing Group in 2021, after meeting them through National Novel Writing Month. When not writing, she is a keen runner and uses her running time to think up even more new story ideas.

S. VALENTINE ASTORIA

Smith is a writer and vampire enthusiast who grew up haunting the graveyards of Hertfordshire. He primarily writes horror and fantasy with his work touching on themes of loneliness and connection, self-realisation, transformation and monstrousness. He has been published in two previous anthologies and featured his work at three consecutive exhibitions run by his other local writing group, The Stortford Scribblers, at his local museum. When he is not writing, he is feeding his ravenous creative appetite with crafts, tabletop roleplaying games, music, photography and drawing.

CALUM DICKINSON

Calum Dickinson is originally from Scotland. He has worked and lived in Hertfordshire for over a decade, training people how to use scientific equipment. From 2009, he has participated and won 15 National Novel Writing Month events, creating stories ranging from Mystery, Fantasy, Steampunk and Historical. Each year he tries a new method for writing or coming up with new concepts and ideas, although puns are often the winning influence. Other than writing, he enjoys bird-watching and bird photography, and has just taken up painting and DIY. Calum can be followed on Instagram @calumbirds

EMILY SIGGERS

Emily Siggers is a twenty-something ex-teacher who lives in Hemel with Lee, her partner of five years (and counting!). She has completed National Novel Writing Month twice, 2023 and exactly 10 years before that in 2013. She mainly writes fantasy and stories within her own world of Gevola which she has spent over ten years creating. She joined The Hertfordshire Writing Group after Nano in 2020 and has been writing with the group ever since. Other than writing, she loves anything textiles and often attends sessions with an ongoing cross stitch project. Emily can be followed on Instagram @essacharl

STUART WAKEFIELD

Stuart is an author and book coach who writes about men who love men. He has been published by Dreamspinner Press and Vine Leaves Press, and his latest book, *Behind the Seams*, was a BookLife Prize Fiction Contest Semifinalist.

Stuart holds an MA in Professional Writing and lives with his husband, pets and too many action figures for a man his age.

EMMA TURNER

Emma Turner is a writer, reader and dreamer originally from the North East of England. After graduating from Cambridge with a degree in Modern Languages, she now works in local government, where she channels her interest in people and places into much more unexpected endeavours: sustainable transport. As a committed climate advocate, Emma's writing commonly features the natural world and our relationship to it, intersectional feminism, and more than just a sprinkling of magic. When she is not writing, she also leads the community group *Create The Future*, where she runs climate writing and art projects. *HOPE,* an anthology featuring creative work from across the globe, was published by Emma and the Create The Future team in 2023.

Also by The Group

SNAPSHORTS: COLLECTED STORIES

A spinster reveals that her life hasn't been as loveless as everyone thought.

A naïve photographer captures the absurd brutality of the Vietnam War.

A model's descent into darkness after a photography session at sea.

A girl. An attic. One mystery. Six photographs. A way out?

Two men. One secret. A photograph that seems to know.

A kidnapped woman has to photograph a dangerous cybertronic creature in order to win back her freedom from a greedy ruler.

From historical fiction to science fiction, mystery to romance, these unforgettable stories will linger with you long after you finish the last page.